Miss Winnie,
There is no way to
measure how much I
appreciate your support.
over the years, your
friendship. Enjoy sharing
Robin's journey!
Peace + Love
Sandi Phillis
(Barbara)
2-2006

FINDING HOME

SANDI HOLLIS

A Novel

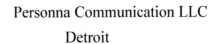

Personna Communication LLC

Detroit

FINDING HOME

Book 1 in the WOMEN OF SHETLAND fiction series

Author: Sandi Hollis

Published by Personna Communication LLC

Detroit, Michigan

Compilation and Formatting: HubBooks/Motown Writers Network

27310 Pilgrim Detroit, MI 48227 | http://HubBooks.biz |

All of the characters in this book are fictitious, and any resemblance to actual persons, living or dead, is purely incidental.

Logo design: Janet Baldwin

Cover Concept: Arno Hoffrichter

Cover Formatting: © 2005 Brenda Lewis

www.ubangigraphics.com

Editor: Heather Thomas

▶▼◀▲

DEDICATION

THIS BOOK IS POSTUMOUSLY DEDICATED TO SISTER JACKIE PAGE. SHE WAS FIRST TO SEE THE WORTH OF ROBIN'S REALITY. ALSO TO AUNTEE ZETTIE BEA, UNCLE BIG JOE, DR. DAUPHINE WALKER-SHIVERS AND PROFESSOR MAXINE POWELL, MY WAYPAVERS.

◄ ▲ ► ▼

ACKNOWLEDGEMENTS

My gratitude to all who are still here and those "gone on" for giving me a rich cache of life-experiences from which to draw, expecially my African "children."

My continued effort, until the characters in this book came to life, was spurred by my monthly critique group, especially Miss Nathalie and Miss Catherine whose voices always whispered into my right ear, never allowing me to rest until the job was done.

A big, big "Thank You" to all who used your valuable time to read. Your recurring feedback-themes sent me scurrying for a more sensory way to say it. Miss Diana, Miss Jackie and Mr. Frederick, you even let me talk it through.

To the rest of my family and friends, "Thank's for being you," still motivating and molding me into the writer I am meant to be.

Finally, Nae, Hansa, Am, Ai and Yuuka, I want you to know how much I appreciate the refreshing energy you shared with me during the final days of this project.

FINDING HOME

SANDI HOLLIS

A Novel

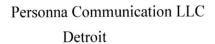 Personna Communication LLC

Detroit

PROLOGUE

You'll understand it better by and by. You jes' hush chil' and don'chu worry."

These words always summoned frustration.

But I don't want to hush and don't worry! I want to understand right now, were words the princess longed to spout in response. But she knew better. No matter how disconcerting her feelings from hearing the words, she knew Godmother must not be addressed in that manner. In the tiny oval kingdom where this story really begins, you just didn't do that.

Why do I always have to wait for some ol' by and by? When will the by and by come, anyhow? Why can't Godmother just tell me right now? What big secret is she trying to hide?

Almost since the procreated bubble was first spotted on the kingdom wall, whoever gave the princess even the teeny-tiniest time was bombarded with a tirade of questions. The questions were ignored as best they could be, since all knew no meaningful answer could be given without first consulting Godmother. When the princess arrived, Godmother, the ideal essence, immediately decreed that every, single thought and movement in the kingdom need have but one purpose: preparing the princess for her imminent journey. No actions could be taken without her blessing.

The most important assignment, Godmother gave to the guardian angels. They were to watch over the princess and keep her safe during what they knew would be a short kingdom stay. Later, the angels had been assigned a more wearisome task. It was their duty alone, to inform the princess of her fate. This was difficult since they knew once the princess was told, everything would change…forever.

When will be the right time to tell her? Where? What words should we use?

While searching for the right time, place and words, the angels still kept their watch and allowed the princess to just…"Be." She could do all the things she loved for as long as she wanted. When she tired, they gently guided her into restful bliss.

What the princess loved more than anything was spending time alone with Godmother. Her favorite time was when Godmother magically sent streams of brightly colored sparkles flickering to and fro as if shooting from Tinkerbell's wand. Sometimes she hurled curlicued swirls, other times graceful zigzags. The lightshow always made the princess giggle uncontrollably. To calm her, Godmother blew streams of multi-colored circles that floated around the princess' head like soldiers marching in precision rows.

Wheeeeeeee! More circles, Godmother, more… pleasssse!

The circles never lasted long. *Pop! Pop! Pop!* No circles, no color…nothing, until Godmother blew out more.

When Godmother wasn't making her magic, she was instructing and explaining. She knew there were many, many things the princess needed to know.

Godmother tells me all sorts of stuff! She tells me about eating and crawling and crying and…Huh, I can ask her about anything I want to!

Well the princess could ask, except about one thing. Whenever Godmother was informing the princess about her parents, who were mysteriously absent from the kingdom, any questioning thought evoked Godmother's tauntingly familiar refrain: *Now you jes' hush chil' and don'chu worry. You'll understand it better by and by.*

Before she could get past her frustration at hearing the words, Godmother was always off to other things leaving the princess in a fuming quandary.

Nothing made the princess happier than Godmother's magic. Nothing made her sadder than Godmother's refrain.

Once, while being lulled into restful bliss, the angels told her about *an outer land where every princess must go...one day.*

Why do I have to leave here? This kingdom is my home. The only thing missing is Mother and Father. I can ask Godmother to bring them here with her magic, can't I?

Instead of offering a reply, the angels continued telling the princess of her fate, completing their assigned task.

When you leave the kingdom, the new land will be your home with your mother and father. We will stay here with Godmother awaiting the next arrival.

What? How can I leave Godmother and the rest of you? Who will watch over me and keep me safe? Who will make me laugh with magic?

Hummmmm. You know about them, too, huh? Why didn't you tell me sooner? I have questions! I want to know how to get to this Mother and Father? Where can I find them? How?

So very tired of all the questions, the angels finally said, *Only Godmother has outside wisdom so ask her.*

Ummph! Now how can I get Godmother to tell me? I guess I'll just have to think of a way...the right way. Hummmmm.

I've got it!

I can catch her in a good mood...Noooooo, Godmother is always in a good mood. Maybe if I am veeeery good and helpful...Nooooo, she won't let me help her. Perhaps if I make her see how much this means to me.... Ah! Maybe if I go to the...Nooooo. Maybe if I....Well there is nothing to do but ask!

Each time the princess asked Godmother even the simplest question about her parents, she heard the familiar refrain: *Now you hush chil'....* After a few tries, she knew it was hopeless and gave up.

Not long after, while floating carefree, a strange beam of light caught the princess' attention. Thinking it might be the angels being playful, she waited for their reveal.

Come out! Come out! Come on over here! I've got something I need to ask you, anyhow!

An eerie silence filled her wait.

All at once, the beam widened. That, scared the princess.

Hurry! Hurry! Come quickly! I think there's something wrong in the wall! You need to come fix it! Hurry! Come quick!

The beam grew brighter and brighter, so bright that the princess felt blinded. Her motions fixed when she saw the claw-like object moving through the beam, heading straight toward her. When the object grabbed, the princess struggled and struggled and struggled and struggled to set herself free. But she was no match for the strength of the claw. Tired and weary she gave in, using her last bit of strength to defensively clamp her eyes shut.

Where are you my angel friends? Why aren't you protecting me? Why aren't you saving me? Don't you see I....

Suddenly, she remembered.

Could it be? Could it be my time to....

Before she finished her thought, the princess felt herself being rapidly drawn through what she knew was the tear in the wall she had seen just before her eyes closed. With a "Swooooosh," she landed in a breezy place filled with strange sounds.

This was the first time the princess had ever heard sounds like these. First time she had felt a breeze. She shuddered. Her body being rubbed over and over and over again, made her shudder even more.

Stop it! Stop it! What are you doing? What are you doing to me?

Godmother! Godmother, help me! Stop them from hurting me! I need you to help me with your magic!

The princess was trying as hard as she could to tell them. But they only heard the familiar, "Whaaaa, whaaaaaaaa, whaaaaaaaaaaaaa," so no one complied.

As soon as the rubbing stopped, the princess cautiously unlocked her eyelids to take a peek. *Ugh!* Another strange object was coming toward her. Quickly, she reshut her eyes, but that did not blot out the squishing sound or suction feelings each time the object made contact with her nose. With every sucking touch, a louder and louder blood-curdling sound filled the room. It took a while before the princess realized she was the source of that yell so incredibly loud, it drowned out all other sounds.

Again, the princess shuddered from the chilly breeze. She was being moved. This time she landed in a hard place. As soon as her tiny body was layed on the surface, it moved downward to accommodate her. When the downward motion stopped, she heard the strange sounds, "Eight pounds, fourteen ounces."

What does that mean? Where am I? If this is the "outer land," how can I look for my mother and father with all these objects grabbing, pulling and sucking?

Hey! Hey! Why can't I understand your sounds? What do they mean? Tell me...tell me something, the princess tried to say using all the energy she could muster.

Only hearing the golden-brown infant's cries, no one replied. They simply fastened every part of her in a wrap so tight she could no longer wiggle or move her arms. In fact, she could barely breathe.

Movement.

Chill. But this time only to her exposed face.

The princess landed in luscious warmth where she felt secure. She opened her eyes. What she saw was amazing. Looking down into hers were eyes brimming with love. When she beheld the smile she had often imagined, joy radiated all over her tiny body. Then she heard the sounds, "Welcome home Robin Marie Talbin, I am your mother" and in a flash, the joyful feelings were deposited deep into her soul.

That set of sounds caught the princess by surprise. She could hardly believe it, but she understood them.

Mother...I am with my mother? I am with my mother like they said?

"Hey, hey look! Look at that, Doc. The little one is smiling and she is only minutes old!"

Robin only seemed to smile. In reality, it was simply the tingling rapture she felt from singing *I am home! I am home! I am home with my mother* over and over in rhythms from nursery rhymes to rumba. With each tune, her joy swelled and swelled until it burst into slight lip quivers.

Though the princess (Oops! Robin) felt tiny tugs of longing for Godmother and the angels, she felt little regret. On that chilly December morning, she knew she was meant to lie peaceful, safe and warm in her mother's arms. But being the curious sort, soon the questions began.

How long will I live in this land? Will it be forever like my best friends said? I know Mother will take care of me, but where is Father? Why isn't he here to watch over me, too? What if he is the one with the magic? If he is, what will I do when I need to laugh?

No one could have guessed how much time would pass before Robin would again happily say, "I am home." There was no one to prepare her for the journey, this time. With the most abstract and colorful imaginings, not Robin herself or even you Dear Reader could have fittingly predicted how her life would be.

Listen, while Robin shares her story. She is counting on you.

PART I

ROE-ROE BEANNIE

▼ ► ▼ ◄

Hey! Whoever you is that hear me while I'm sittin' up here in this Chinaberry tree talkin' to you, 'cause I ain' got nobody else I can talk to. Don'chu go 'way an' leave me, too! I got to talk to somebody. Needs to know 'bout some stuff.

You listenin'? You gotta listen real good, 'cause if people hear me talkin' to you, they gon' say I got a lit'l touch in my head. You know what I mean? What lit'l girl want people to say that 'bout'er?

I <u>can</u> talk to you, cain't I? I tried talkin' to some other folks, but I could tell they tol'. Now, I'm real scary to try an' talk to anybody, 'cause I got lotsa secret stuff I wanna say.

Okay, I'm gon' try you and see.

Here go.

Naaaaw…I don' know.

You won' tell, will you?

Okay, I'll tell you. But firs' lemme tell you this:

Now I know you s'pose to feel good where yo' home is. With all the family 'roun in the house where you was born, it seem lack a lit'l girl oughtta feel good. But way back, far as I remember, there was always somewhere else I oughtta be, but I don' know where, ra't now. Somethin' else I oughtta be doin', too, but I don' know what that is ra't now either.

It jes' happen I was born in Shetland. I heard talk that my mamma and my daddy was two teenagers jes' foolin' 'roun' seein' what was what. I neeeever heard where they firs' met each other at and my mind cain't even picture how they got to makin' me. Maybe they jes' tryin' to make a lit'l magic, have a lit'l fun…or somethin'.

Wonder where my daddy went when the laughin' was over? What kinda lit'l girl is it that ain't got no daddy to see after her? I ain' got no Godmother to make ev'rythang alright lack Miss Cinderella in the story book. Ain't even got no brother or sister to play with, neither. I ain't got nobody.

You still there?

Sho' glad you is!

Listen.

Yesterday I heard my cousins say, "There ain't <u>no</u> place you can have fun in Shetland." I hear'em sass grown people and say that all the time. When it's gittin' night, my bad-girl cousins put on they taffeta, wide-skirt dress and them nylon stockin's with the seam up the back and go waaaaaay down to Pego to try an' have fun.

Wonder why they go waaaaay down there? I hope they don' have a car wreck comin' home one night lack them White boys did. Hope they body don' fly out the window in the corn field with both they shoes still in the car. Sho' hope nobody find'em dead on the ground with they neck broke, 'cause they jes' tryin' to have a lit'l fun. Maybe one a these days, they can have some fun ra't here lack I do time to time.

► ▼ ▲ ◄

Ev'ry once in a while I have a whole lotta fun ra't here in Shetland. My bes' fun is when I clam' up in this Chinaberry tree where I can talk to you and see Paree, way, way down yonder. I have a lit'l fun playin' with my pals, too.

> *Where do all the spooks live?*
> *Down in Paree!*
> *Where do all the spooks live?*
> *Down in Paree!*
> *Where do all the spooks live?*
> *Down in Paree! Down in Paree!*
> *Where they hands go…(clap, clap)*
> *And they feet go…(stomp, stomp)*
> *And they hips go…(wiggle, wiggle, wiggle)*
> *All night long.*

My pals and me, we always try to play Spooks in Paree at recess time. We got to go where teachers cain't see, 'cause they git us when we wiggle.

They always say, "Stop it! What's wrong with ya'll? Why ya'll doin' that nasty dance? You jes' got the devil in you, that's all!"

Them teachers act lack we doin' somethin' wrong, but we jes' havin' fun. Wigglin' hips don' hurt nobody…Do it?

Sometime I thank maybe my cousins tell the truth, though. When we git caught, it sho' feel jes' lack it ain't no fun here. I bet you could have many times the fun somewhere else.

I can wiggle the bes'. That's prob'ly 'cause when I wiggle it make me feel all warm inside. When the others gather 'round me clappin' and laughin', my hips jes' tight'n up and wiggle real fast. Sometimes I be scared though. 'Cause when I be the bes', it make Freda Jean Crosby mad. I be scared she gon' tell.

Wonder if the devil gon' git me for the way I wiggle? Prob'ly naaaw. 'Cause then he would have to git all my pals and some grown ladies I see sometime. He prob'ly cain't carry all us off.

Let me tell you 'bout my second bes' fun. That's when Uncle James ask me if I wanna go "Over Town." I know a few thangs then: I'm gon' git to lick my tongue way down in that good ol' cold, sweet ice cream layin' up in that crunchy cone and taste that good ol' sweet car-a-mel it have all over the top and runnin' down the sides. The other thang is that I git to 'cross the river. I cain't wait to jump on the back seat in Uncle James' ol' Chevy and roll them windows down so the wind can start blowin' in my face, ticklin' my eyes.

Whoever I be playin' with, cain't wait either. We race to clam'up in that ol' car and tussle to see who git to sit nex' to the window. You need the seat by the window so you can see the outside real good and be firs' one to claim.

"That's my blue car! That's my white house! That's my brown dog!"

We play 'til we come to the Shetland bridge, then I always git quiet. If the others ever wonder why, they never ask. I think maybe they have they own stuff goin' on in they head lack me, 'cause they git quiet too.

Cain't nothin' jes' hook up to the sky, can it? The Shetland bridge-sho' look lack it do. If you jes' look up at the top, the bridge-poles look that way when you goin' cross. But I know it really cain't.

Know what? If I look down jes' at the right part on this one bridge side, I see the 'lectric plant with all them windows, go "bang, crash" ra't into the bridge.

Fooled ya! It don't do that for real, it jes' seem lack it.

If the bridge and the plant did crash, I know I would hear them go, "Pow yow, pow yow" and see a whole lotta squiggley, squiggle fire shoot up everywhere lack you thank might come out if a fairy was to wave a magic wand at'chu. I see them squiggles in my mind a lot at night when I'm almos' sleep.

Why I keep seeing that, I wonder? I'll be glad when I find somebody who could tell me. Do you know? Maybe we can talk about that after I git lotsa other stuff said.

Anyhow, when I was real, real lit'l, maybe goin' on three or five, goin' 'cross the bridge was lack bein' at the circus. The wind made some "swhooshing" sounds ev'ry time we pass a pole. Then you could hear the water go "swiiiiiissssssssh, shou-yow" when it be comin' over the dam and fallin' way down on the rocks. Then the plant go "hummmmmmm." Them sounds all put together with the "flick, flick, flick" all them bridge-poles have the sun doin', made me feel lack I was ridin' on the, the...ummmmm, you know the ride with the horses...the merry-go-round. Yea, that's what they call it!

Ummph, a circus ain't been 'round Shetland in a long time. It's been so long 'til I cain't really remember what all the rides call. But I can still almost smell the popcorn and taste that good ol' cotton candy.

I wanna tell you somethin' I ain't neeeeeeever told nobody, 'cause they may thank I'm coo coo. I really, really hope you won't tell this:

One day when I was on the bridge, I got this funny feelin' that came all over my body, theeen I saw myself grow way big and reach way, way down through the 'lectric plant windows and grab them sparkly 'lectric-bolts that it make inside. The first thang I had to do was figger out jes' how to make them bolts quiet down so they wouldn' hurt me. Thought they couldn' hurt me if I found a way to not have so much water goin' down on the rocks an' into them big ol' wheel-cups that took it an' po'ed it in the plant.

All of a sudden,…"zap!" My way big body was layed backward on the wood at the Shetland river dam top. Then, "zip-zap," I started changin' to a whole lotta me's. All them me's stretched side-by-side 'cross the whole river dam with all our arms locked up to each other real tight. That way, if we don' want much water to go down to the plant, we jes' tight'n up our arms to make a lit'ler hole. The mo' tighter our arms, the lit'ler the water that could go. If we wanted that river water to not go to the plant at all, but to the big ol' tank on the side, we turnt all our bodies a lit'l and swung our legs away from one 'nother.

All that stuff put a tingle feelin' all over my inside. Lef' it there a while, too.

A long time after that day, whenever I would cross the bridge I jes' kep'on thankin' and sayin', "I am super power! S w i sh-sh-sh! Splash-sh-sh-sh! H-u-m-m-m-m-m-m!"

Sometime I still feel that way. When I do, I jes' thank how I got to do somethin' real special when I grow up lack Auntee Bertha say. Mosta the time, Uncle James' car be done gone clear 'cross the bridge befo' I stop thankin' 'bout it an' I ain't even got to peep down on the other bridge side to see if I could see any scary mill people.

Wonder what kinda special thang I can do when I git grown? What you thank? I was thankin' I could be President, but Uncle James all the time tellin' Cousin Shudda he gon' be President when he grow up. He tell me to go to the kitchen and help Auntee Bertha so I can learn how to cook real good and make some man a good wife. Somehow, that jes' don' feel good. I know I could be a real good President. Cousin Shudda ain' even as strong as me. An' he sho cain't talk good as me. I am the superpower! Why don' Uncle James see that?

Oh, guess I better finish tellin' you 'bout the bridge stuff befo' you stop lis'nin' an' go on off somewhere, huh?

When we goin' back home and jes' befo' we 'bout to leave the bridge, I always peep down to see if I see any people I know that work at the mill that's way down on the river edge. I don' look long, 'cause I don' know but a few people that work down there. Most people I know live on Mr. Grace place and do some sharetoppin'...sharecoppin'...or somethin' lack that. Well anyhow, I know they work hard all day in Mr. Grace fields.

◄ ▲ ▼ ►

My cousins say it's a good thang they work for Mr. Grace, 'cause "you always have eeeenough." They say if they mamma "run short, Mr. Grace carry her." When it come time to pay, Mr. Grace don' charge no extra lack other bosses do. My cousins tell me all the time, "Boss Grace sho' is a good White man."

Almos' ev'ry mornin', all eighta my cousins git up early so they can be out on the road to wait for Lem (my other cousin) to pick'em up in Mr. Grace truck and take'em to big ol' cotton fields. It don' matter if they tired and sleepy lack some of'em be after stayin' 'til late in Paree at Mr. Jake's Honkey Tonk, the juke joint they go to down there when they don' wanna go to Pego. They be tired from doin' that ol' nasty dance they call the Booty Green and drankin' that white light'nin'. I hear'em talkin' 'bout it. Ra't now, they gotta work all the days, except a half-day on Saturday and all day Sunday. They jes' be workin' and sweatin' all day long so they "make sure all Boss Grace cotton git to that gin."

Even though they don' have to work on church day, my cousins still don' go to church. They might as well be gittin' the cotton ready for the gin or juke jointin', since the devil gon' git'em anyhow.

Know what? That ol' cotton gin jes' sit, mos'ly. It jes' sit and wait for cotton plants to be planted that it know gon' be lined up in a lotta long, long rows. When the cotton stalks grow tall, they gon' git greeeat biiig ol' white blooms an' some big ol' bubs, too. When the bubs be closed and hard and green, ev'ry one of'em jes' hang there on them stalks. But after a while, them hard ol' bubs turn different. They open up into bows where you can see the cotton on the inside. Ev'ry open bub jes' hang there stuck together at the bottom lack a hand, theeeeen

16

the top spread open and look lack five or six fangers handin' you some balled-up fluffy, white stuff.

Where you from? You ever seen a cotton bow or seen people pick cotton?

Maybe you ain't or maybe you is. But let me tell you this, jes' 'cause I want you to know ev'rythang real clear:

Them cotton-bows might be kinda lack a hand, but they hand don' look lack mine. They got points where they fangers end, where I got nails. They fanger firs' come out from the bow bottom kinda wide, theeeeen go up to skinny lit'l ends all sharp and stickly jes' lack the head that's on a sewin' machine needle.

While the cotton plants git grown an' ready, my cousins be makin' an' fixin' the sacks they gon' use for pickin'. They make ev'ry sack-strap jeessss' long enough for how tall ev'rybody is, ya know. That way, where the sack open will be a good spot to git the cotton in it the easies' and quickes'. When they fi'nta pick the cotton, them straps go over they heads, 'cross they shoulders an' they ches' so them sacks can be dragged up and down, up and down ev'ry row.

My cousins that make an' fix the sacks, want to make sho' ev'rybody pick they hunderd pounds eeeev'ry day. Don' want nobody to miss not one five dollars come Friday.

When I go to the fields, I watch my cousins real close. They stop at ev'ry cotton plant, bend over they back jeeees' a little, make they fangers into a crawfish claw, then push'em down into ev'ry bow to git out all the cotton.

The points from them bow-fangers stick a whole, whole lot. By the time my cousins knock off from pickin' and head for Mr. Grace truck, they fangers have dry blood speckles all over'em. Some be on they hands, too. Even on the back. Aaaaand, some be on they clothes where they be done wipe.

"Hey! Come on let's go," Cousin Lem always hollerin'. "I got to git ya'll home so I can git some salve on my fangahs!"

They Grandma Alice make salve 'cause she ain' got no money to buy Red Top oin'ment from Mr. Ryan sto'. It cost too much.

Wonder when I ain't there, do my cousins cuss when they prick they fangers lack I hear some ol' folks do when they hurt they hand? I hope…no. 'Cause the devil sho'ly gon' git'em if they cuss. Send'em straight on down to that "ol' lake a fire." If they do, I hope somebody can do somethin' to make'em stop befo' it be too late.

Ev'ry day, all the time when my cousins send cotton to the gin, they weigh it and wash it real clean, then send it over to the mill. The mill people make that cotton be big ol' thread-spools and long wrappin' cloth-bolts that big ol' trucks carry ev'rywhere.

Can I do that kinda work when I git grown? Naaaaaw! Pickin' a hunderd pounds a day and workin' in the mill ain' special. Besides, I don' want nobody lookin' down from the bridge seein' me lookin' lack a ghost. Don' wanna eeeven talk to you 'bout that now.

◄▲▼►

Two days a week, Cousin Lem take my cousin I lacks the bes' that's sixteen, to help her mamma in the "bighouse." Cousin Sissy and Auntee Vee clean up ev'rythang, pick, cut up and cook greens, beans and okree, theeen wash and iron all the clothes for Mr. Grace, Miss Grace and them three ol' ugly, crazy chil'en they got.

See, that's why I'm glad I fin'ly got somebody to talk to that won' tell. If I say that kinda stuff to anybody else, they be sayin', "Now Roe-Roe, you know better than sayin' that." I'm sho' gon' be glad when I can go where nobody gon' stop me from sayin' what I wanna say! I can't even say how much I hate ev'rybody callin' me Roe-Roe and Roe-Roe Beannie.

"My name is Robin! R-O-B-I-N!!" (Oooops), I said that kinda loud, didn't I?

Know what? Cousin Sissy is the veeery best. She all pretty lack a movie star and all tall lack a pine tree, but when she walk, the way her body and hair move make me thank about the weepin' willow tree my play house under in the back yard. When some wind blow, Cousin Sissy's long hair jes' be blowin' firs' one way then the other jes' lack them willow switches…unless she pin it down or put a head scarf on her head.

Cousin Sissy is real sweet and kind…and bright, too. She can read an' write an' ev'rythang!

"Roe-Roe, did I tell you 'bout the room in Mr. Grace house that got books on a whole wall," Cousin Sissy say one day.

Sho' glad Cousin Sissy know I lack books. Ev'ry since I was real lit'l and could look at the pictures, I been lackin'em. I hear when I was real, real lit'l, I use to carry a book 'round under my arm all the time.

When Cousin Sissy tol' me 'bout that room, I couldn' believe it. I didn't know to wonder then, but now I wonder with the way folks always workin' here in Shetland, why would anybody have a room where the whole wall ain' got nothin' but books? When do anybody, but Miss. Grace have time to read'em? Aaaaand, "Miss Grace cain't read." That's what Cousin Sissy had tol' me one day, laughin'.

When I could, Cousin Sissy took me to sneak in and see that room. Seein' all them books...well at firs' I jes' went, "Wow, Wow" over and over and over. Couldn' say nothin' else. Jes' thought, *How long would it take me to read all them books, if I could read lack I want to learn?* I knowd that even if I could read real, real good and real, real fas' the way Cousin Sissy do, it would still prob'ly take me 'bout...uuuuh, a billion, trillion years to read'em all. An' by the time I got through, I would be old lack that Mr. Rip VanWinkle man Cousin Sissy had read to me 'bout. Maybe ol' lack that real, real ol' man they talk about in Sunday School, Mr. Madu, nawww, Mathu...well you know who I'm talkin' 'bout, don'chu?

The Graces got to be the smartes' people in the whole wide world. Maybe that's why they rich and got my cousins livin' on they place and workin' for'em.

Hummmmmm.

It took me a long time to take my eyes off them books. But after while, I started wonderin' jes' how somebody made them shelves go 'round that big ol' radio standin' on the floor ra't in the mid'l. It was on the same wall the books was on. At firs', I thought that big ol' radio was a Rockola lack what me an' Couisin Shudda saw in Mr. Jake's honkey tonk befo' we got caught sneakin'.

When I git grown and have me a house, I'm gon' be rich and have a room with books on eeeev'ry wall. Maybe I'll have to put the chairs ra't in the mid'la the room, 'steada on they own wall lack Miss Grace got.

'Ventu'ly, I let my eyes see all the room. Two big ol' brown, puffy-up chairs was on both the wall ends where the bookshelfs stop. There was a real tall light nex' to each one of'em, sittin' on the floor. On the wall over the chairs, there was some big pictures of some men ridin' horses and one was holdin' up a flag.

The flag look lack somebody took a big ol' white sheet an' sewed a X ra't in the mid'la the big red square that was at the up corner part, by the top, nex' to the pole. That X had thirteen stars in it. I counted ev'ry one. At firs' I thought it was fo'teen, but then I saw I was countin' the mid'l star two times. There was a wide, red strip at the very other flag end, too.

In one picture, the man in front was holdin' the flag way up high. In the other picture the man jes' had the flag stuck in the horse saddle. Maybe he stuck it there so he could use both his hands to make his horse "gee" and "haw."

Wonder who they is? They must be some special soldiers, 'cause they up on the wall in them picture frames. Maybe they special 'cause they rode in on them pretty black horses to save the world from the bad people.

Ra't then, that room made me know I had to git real smart, so I could be rich an' have a liberium…liberia, or whatever Cousin Sissy call that room. I cain't thank about the name ra't now.

"Roe-Roe! Roe-Roe! Come here quick," I heard Cousin Sissy whisper real loud. I ran to the kitchen lack grease lignt'nin', so Miss Grace wouldn' ketch me where I didn't belong.

Wonder where it is I do belong? I really want to know, 'cause it seem ev'rywhere here in Shetland, people don' want me to be.

Listen…I'll tell you a secret if you promise me you won' tell.

Ya promise?

Well you know what Cousin Sissy did this one time?

Now remember you promise!

Cousin Sissy stole a book from Mr. Grace room and gave it to me. My heart almos' died.

Oh, Jesus, Cousin Sissy! Mr. Grace'll chop yo' hands off with his big ol' hoe. Maybe shoot you with that shotgun he carry 'round.

I was real scared Granny might see that book and ask me where I got it, so I hid it waaaaay under my mattress. I watched ev'ry day to see if Cousin Sissy got home alright.

"Roe-Roe, we need a book so I can teach you how to read real good," Cousin Sissy tol' me. She taught me too.

When I firs' started learnin', Cousin Sissy used to write down firs' two words, then three words an' sometimes more than that. Theeeeeen, she spelt out an' said each one of'em r-e-a-l s-l-o-w. Theeeeen, she have me spell out and say the word over an' over 'til I know it by hard. Ev'rytime when Cousin Sissy was readin' me a story and come to a word we had practiced, she stop readin' and point to me so I could say it 'steada her. I was a real fas' learner. In a lit'l while, I could read all the words in that whole, stole book all by myself.

Yep, Cousin Sissy is the bes', alright. Know what though? If I was grown and she was workin' for me, I would never send her to the fields and have her workin' in the house lack Mr. Grace do. I would jes' always have her readin' books and writin' them pretty stories lack she do sometime. She even write some "poams," "pomes," or somethin' lack that.... Anyhow, all I know is when she write one with me in it, it make me feel real, real special. Listen to this one.

A lit'l star is born, an'

Roe Roe pluck it from the sky.

To give her path some light,

When lots of darkness is nigh.

Ain' that pretty? Why you thank Mr. Grace don' see how smart Cousin Sissy is? Why won't he let her do all the good readin' and writin' stuff she know how to do real good? She could prob'ly teach Miss Grace to read, even.

Huh, with that kinda treatment, maybe Shetland ain' where Cousin Sissy oughtta be either. Mr. Grace ain' even tryin' to let her be her <u>real</u> self. When I git to the 'moanin' bench' Sunday, I have to pray for Cousin Sissy real hard. Pray that Mr. Grace eyes see better, too."

▲ ▼ ► ◄

Ev'ry once in a while, I beg and beg and I git to go a whole day to the fields with all my cousins. Ev'ry time I do, Mr. Grace don' lack it. He see me and send his son "bun dic" or "bunda dick," or whatever my cousins call him while they be snigglin' under they breath.

"G-a-l g-i-t y-o b-l-a-c-k a-s-s o-u-d-d-a m-y f-i-e-l's s-o d-e-s-e c-h-i-l-l-u-n-s k-i-n g-i-t s-o-m-e c-o-t'n p-i-c-k-t."

Mr. BD always say stuff in that long stretched out talk lack White folks in Shetland talk. Then he walk ra't up real close to me, he pucker his lips real tight and spit a long, black squirt off to the side. He look in my face and make a "shissss'in' sound.

Who he thank he trickin'? Who he thank he scarin'?

Mr. BD be all red in his face lack them pickle beets I love. He cain't talk outta his whole mouth, jes' his lip sides. Need to use mosta his lip to hold his big ol' snuff wad.

"Jes' don't pay him no mind," my cousins always say. "Jes' keep on doin' what you be doin'" It work, too. When he come yellin', I chop. He yell. I pick. Befo' long, Mr. BD jes' turn his fat body 'round and walk off, makin' that big ol' bundle down where his private is, shake from side-to-side lack that Jello Cousin Sissy showed me she fix for Miss Grace that time. That bundle go "jiggle, jiggle" ev'ry time he make a step. He be spitin' out a buncha cuss words and ugly names for me while my cousins be bent over doin' all kindsa thangs tryin' not to laugh out loud.

Though I ain't done nothin', why I keep on feelin' lack one a them "starnatal fools" I hear the ol' folks call somebody that done acted up reeeal bad?

Every time after Mr. BD leave, I laugh with my cousins, but jes' say to myself one mo' time, "I ain' neeeever gon' work in no White folks fields when I git grown. Besides, wouldn't have no time to read.

I don' understand why my cousins act happy, havin' to put up with this kinda mess all the time, 'specially for that lit'l money they git. I sho' don' know how they can even be alright. Don' they see the difference when our kin come to visit dressed to kill? Shoooot. I bet up North, my other kin make a lotta money teachin' kids and nursin' sick folk. I know them that make big ol' cars do! The firs' time Uncle Charles and Auntee Peggy came, I saw how sharp they looked, heard them talk and knew I had to leave Shetland. Got to figger out jes' where I'm gon' git the money at, though.

Besides not workin' in the fields, I know I cain't never come walkin' outta my work lookin' lack a cotton-mill ghost. Since I'm a girl, nobody gon' let me drag and lift them great big ol' boxes on the Company Sto' dock where other folks I know work. Aaaaaan'…I ain't never seen no Negro be a saleslady lack what I want to be. Shucks, ev'ry time I go to the sto' an' look at thangs, them White salesladies jes' watch me lack they thank me and whoever I come with gon' steal somethin'. They know me. They know I don' steal. Who they thank want to have Sheriff Black Bart git'em and put'em in jail? Who they thank want the devil to git'em? Not me. Naaaaaaw buddy, not me.

Don' nobody else thank this, but I know it: One day, somebody gon' come and take me far, far away to my "real" home. Maybe it will be my daddy.

"Yes Ma'am, yes Ma'am I'm comin'!"

'Scuse me, I have to go see what Granny want. But, I'll try to be ra't back. I got to figger this thang out an' talkin' to you help me.

► ◄ ▲ ▼

"Granny, you jes' want to know if I'm gonna stay up in the tree all night? It a-i-n't e-v-e-n n-e-a-r d-a-r-k, yet…Ma'am."

Now why she call me down to ask me that? She know I know I'm gon' sleep in the house with her and the rest of 'em. I thought she called me 'cause supper was ready or somethin'.

Do you know that Granny, Mamma and me live in the house with Uncle Ray and his wife? Altogether, we have as fine a house as Mr. Grace do, 'cept we ain' got a…uuh…whatever Cousin Sissy call that room 'specially built for books.

I got to remember that word! Got to!

Each family got our own kitchen, our own bedrooms, even our own livin' room. You wouldn' say we all was sharin' if you didn' count the roof up yonder on the house top an' the inside outhouse at the back that all us use. See, Uncle Ray is what they call a "master plummer." That means, on the weekend when he ain' workin' at the hospital, White folks pay him to fix toilets, sinks and stuff. At the backa the house, Uncle Ray built us a outhouse, inside, with a sink for washin' up, a tub for takin' a bath and ev'rythang!

"Roe-Roe, that somethin' special we oughtta thank God for," Granny say. "How many a yo' kin you know with a inside toilet?"

"None."

Do you know what my Granny look lack? Well…let me tell you so you know when you see her.

My Granny look lack the lady on the grits box, but I'm glad she don' wear no head rag on her head. Granny wear her hair in two braids through the week and lotsa curls on Sunday, so no need. Don' paint her lips red, neither.

"Remember Roe-Roe, only Jezebel women paint they lips."

"Yes Ma'am Granny," I always say back.

Wonder if Aunt Jemima really is a Jezebel woman? She look real sweet. I sho' would lack to meet her. If she is Jezebel, I need to tell her to git saved ra't now so the devil won' git her and put her in the "lake a fire".

Shoot, they prob'ly jes' painted Aunt Jemima picture that way. She prob'ly a Godfearing woman jes' lack Granny. Folks always tryin' to trick somebody.

Granny jes' be by herself most time. Hardly ever see her laugh. I guess she don' want to make herself laugh by herself and git people thankin' she coo-coo lack Miss Janet.

When Miss Janet come walkin' by the house, even if it's ten times in one day, she always say the same thing: "Reck'n it gwhy be anothah day?" I ain' never heard her say nothin' else. That's what let people know she coo coo.

How Miss Janet git that way, I wonder? I bet she know Shetland ain' where she oughtta be and jes' keep on stayin' here. If it was her home, it wouldn' make her "coo coo," now would it?

Do you thank if I keep stayin' here in Shetland I'm gon' end up coo coo lack Miss Janet?

Huh?

Oh that's right, you don' talk back. You jes' listen.

Let me tell you this…

Eeeev'ry now and then, I see Granny's pretty, black, roun' face crinkle up to somethin' that look kinda lack a smile. It ain't the kind that put some light on her face, but one that look hard to make.

Ya think maybe it hurt her lips?

Wonder why Granny don' smile much? She got pretty, white teeth. You would thank if God love her lack she say He do, He would want her to smile all the time. I know I smile ev'ry time I thank how much Granny love me. Could it be she sad 'cause she stuck here livin' in Shetland, too? I hope she ain't gon' go coo coo. 'Cause if she do, I know I have to stay here and take care of 'er an' I sho' don' want to have to do that.

Now this what I thank. Maybe Granny don' smile 'cause she work too much. I don' see nobody laugh much when they work 'cep' the men at the Company Sto'. They have them big 'ol wide smile-grins on they face when they loadin' them trucks lack they loadin' up a present they done give folks for Christmas. I don' know why they grin so much. All that work cain't make you happy. If it did, Granny would be happy all the time. Ev'ry day she jes' be cookin', workin' in the garden, cannin', or bakin' somethin'. When I ask Granny why she be workin' all the time, I hear the same ol' thang, e-v'-r-y, s-a-n-g-l-e time: "Now you hush chil' and don'chu worry. You gon' understand it bedder by an' by." Ev'ry time she say that, it make me real, real mad, but I know better than to let on.

Why I have to wait to know why Granny work so hard? Why can't I understand ra't now? Is it lack cousin Sissy say, 'Work is what you do when you be the granny in the house? If it is, why don' Granny jes' tell me that?

Granny don' jes' always make me mad. Sometimes she make me feel lack I be in jes' the right place. Know when? When she be bakin' her good ol' cakes an' let me lick the bowl.

There I be sittin' on the back porch. My fangers stuck down in that big ol' bowl, whirlin' 'em 'round the sides so they git filled up with that good ol' batter. I hold my hand up so the batter can drip ra't down in my mouth, I know Granny be makin' them cherubs I see in the Sunday School book play they harps. I can hear'em. I keep up with what they be playin' with my dippin', whirlin' and drippin' an' I don' stop 'til the bowl is clean.

"Roe-Roe, that's enough. I wanna use that bowl again."

I stop when Granny tell me, too.

I been lovin' bein' with Granny since I was real, real lit'l and she firs' had me helpin' her work in the garden. For a long time befo' that, I felt lack I had been lef'. But lack magic, I didn' feel lef' when I was up an' down ev'ry row with Granny while she chop "dem ol' devil weeds." I would pick'em up and put'em in the weed pile. Had a lit'l sack jes' lack the one my cousins use when they pickin' cotton. When my sack got full, I drug it clear to the weed pile.

"Miss Roe-Roe Beannie, you a real good helper."

"Thank you Granny."

I looooove my granny. Ev'rybody else must love her too. They always askin' her to do stuff with'em. On Saturday, somebody always ask Granny to go Over Town. She jes' say, "Wait 'til I git my shoes." Then, she put her shoes on an' dab on some special granny potion an' away she go.

That's right, you don' know 'bout Granny potion.

Granny potion is kinda lack somebody took some juice from "scoffin dimes, scopin dines"…or somethin' lack that. Anyhow, they put that juice together with big ol' ripe green plum juice and stirred in some caramel with a lit'l squeezed lemon juice and dab a vanilla flavor. Ev'ry time I git close to Granny, I breathe up my nose real fast, but real quiet so she won' know I'm sniffin' her.

Since when I was real lit'l, I never could wait 'til Sunday when Granny dab some potion on me. She would pick up off the dresser, her lit'l blue bottle with the flowers cut deep in both sides an' give two squeezes to that lit'l ol' pink rubber ball hangin' on the top. Ev'ry time the potion spray out on Granny's hands, she dab it on my dress in a different place.

Wonder why she don' put the potion on my wris' and behind my ears lack I see her do on her?

I would walk around jes'breathin' in and out, smelling potion on my dress. After a little while though, I couldn' smell it on me, no more. So I'd git real close to Granny and do my quiet sniffin'. When I smell that smell, there is no place else I wanna be.

Help me figger somethin' out about Granny I always wanted to know: How did she git to makin' all her chil'en without no daddy? If I git the answer to that maybe it'll let me know 'bout Mamma an' me.

Oh I have to remember, you don' talk back. Since you don', I guess I have to keep on tryin' to figger thangs out by myself. But it sho' help to talk to you.

▼ ► ◄ ▲

It weren't 'til the day I heard my grandfather was dead and had been buried in the ground that I started figgerin' some stuff out.

"Granny, look! A car is comin' up the road!"

"Unmmm hummm!"

That day, soon as Granny's eyes seent the shiny, gray car comin', she put the peas she was shellin' in the pan down on the flo' and went in the house real fas'. Scared me at firs', but then I thought maybe she smelt somethin' burnin' on the stove, or somethin'. I got to sniffin' real hard, but didn' smell a thang. Wondered some after that, but jes' decided to sit there on the steps watchin' the car,

It sho' would be nice if that car was comin' to take me somewhere.

I was really surprised when the car got close. Uncle Ray was drivin' it. When he firs' drove up in the driveway, Granny came back to the door an' I saw this look on her face. It look lack hurt, vexation, and lotsa sadness all rolled up in one. Granny was lookin' mo' hurt and vexed when Uncle Ray started tellin' her thangs about Grandfather. I remember that day real good.

I got a real grandfather? I don' have to make up no grandfather when the others talk about what they did with they Papa?

Now I need you to help me figger out how I can tell my pals! I always told'em my grandfather couldn't come to Shetland. People would steal all his gold and stuff. When you can, help me know what you thank I need to do some kinda way.

Seein' Granny's look, I knew this girl oughtta be quiet and keep out her way. So I jes' kep' my eyes an' ears as wide open as I could. Mouth? Shut. It prob'ly was lookin' lack I had two big ol' cabbage heads for eyes and great big ol' collard leaves for ears. But that way, I could watch and hear what was goin' on.

What do that mean, I thought when Uncle Ray firs' started talkin'. *I gotta remember so I can ask Cousin Sissy. Who is Uncle Ray callin' "Daddy?" What? I gotta remember that word. "Artopsi.," Gotta ask Cousin Sissy if that's a word.*

I finally figgered out that Uncle Ray was talkin'' 'bout Grandfather.

I guess I oughtta tell you Grandfather's story, huh? 'Cause you don' know nothin' 'bout'im, do you? Well here it go:

Way in a lit'l town up North…

'Til I heard what Uncle Ray say, I didn' even know they had lit'l towns up North. I thought they jes' had big ol' cities lack the ones I saw in the magazine Cousin Chichi lef' when she came for Christmas.

Anyhow as I was sayin'…

Way in a lit'l town up North, my grandfather had died, dead from bein' stabbed with a knife twelve times. That's t-w-e-l-v-e., twelve. He wasn' doin' nothin' but jes' sittin' in the car with his new girlfriend, from what I heard. His ol' girlfriend who did the stabbin', got real jealous.

I don' see why that firs' girlfriend got so jealous lack that, 'specially since Cousin Sissy told me she was his girlfriend when he was still husband to Granny. She was the reason Grandfather was up in Tannica in the firs' place. That firs' girlfriend had took him to Tannica and kep'im there to live with her and her Uncle Ron.

Seem to me it be lack Cousin Sissy say, "a turn aroun' is a fair hit…a fair game"…well somethin' lack that. Huh, Granny didn't git so mad that she followed them and did Grandfather or that firs' girlfriend harm. Granny jes' turnt to Jesus and He made it alright for her…, leas' I thank He did.

Wonder if somethin' bad will happen to me when I leave Shetland for good lack what happen to Grandfather?

Uncle Ray had jes' come from the court trial where Grandfather's girlfriend got plenty prison time. Granny got some thangs call his …ummmmmmmm …"eeeffects," I thank. The law say she git'em, 'cause she ain' never stop bein' his wife. The gray car was one of'em.

How could you be a wife to somebody and never, ever see'em?

The gray car jes' set ra't over there in the driveway where it sittin' now, day in and day out. All the time, it jes' set there. I don' know why. For a long time, it was lack nobody could touch any of Grandfather's thangs. But one day, I saw Uncle Ray put Grandfather's almos' new wallet in his pocket. I saw him burn up Grandfather's clothes, too. He say he burnt'em 'cause they had holes in'em and places where blood had got dry. He pro'bly did it 'cause he had jes' got married and was movin' to Virginia and didn't want to take'em with'im. He knew better than leave'em with Granny.

Hey, maybe I can go to Virginia to live with Uncle Ray and his new wife. I am real good. Wouldn't be no trouble.

Naw, I better stay here with Granny so she have somebody to talk to lack I have you.

Nobody said nothin' else 'bout Grandfather that I heard. Granny never said a word to me 'bout'im and started actin' much lack he never was. But I knew better.

After Uncle Ray lef', I started sneakin' in the car to practice drivin' in my mind. Ev'ry time I did, I would open my hands real wide and put'em ra't on the only real thang I knew 'bout Grandfather: the place where his blood drop down on the car seat and lef' big ol' spots. After I open my two hands up real, real wide, I would slowly rub the spots back and forth, back and forth, then close my eyes real, real tight and try to picture in my mind how Grandfather felt when that knife split his skin open and crashed through his bones straight to his heart.

Was he scared? 'Though a man ain' s'pose to, you thank he cried?

Do you be thankin' it strange that a lit'l girl from Shetland say "grandfather" 'steada "grandpa" or "papa?" You jes' gotta remember...thangs got mixed up. I jes' happen to be born here. But I'm really, really a princess from a land where...well, I don' know ra't now. In the fairytale book I read, it say a princess got a "grandfather" an' "grandmother." Been callin' him Grandfather ev'ry since.

▲ ▼ ◄ ►

I call my grandmother "Granny," jes' to make her happy. I know if she was at church 'round the "saints" and I would call her "Grandmother," them saints would be askin' her, "Laud wheah did dat chil' git dat hi'-fallutin' talk from?" Cousin Sissy say she heard'em say they cain't understand why Granny didn' put Mamma out when she fount out she was havin' a baby and didn' have no husband.

I thank they call that "fondication," "fonalation" or somethin' lack that.

One day when I was at church and back in the last cubby on the toilet usin' it, I heard Miss Carrie and Miss Cindy sayin', "…and chil' she ev'n heppin' herda raise dat bastard chil' a her'n too." I thought they was talkin' 'bout me and Granny, but I was sho' when I came out. Miss Carrie took one look at me and yelt, "Do Jesus." Miss Cindy jes' stood there with her mouth wide open lack somebody had scared'er.

Back then, I couldn' read good enough to read the book Granny had on the bookshelf that tol' what words mean. I waited 'til I saw Cousin Sissy to ask what "bastard" meant. But I knew a few thangs ra't off: a bastard is a bad thang and even the saints knew I was somewhere I weren't s'pose to be.

Why the saints talk bad lack that, I wonder? Don't God keep they mouth holy? Keep they tongue so it talk clean? If He don't, should I reeeally be trustin' Him to take care of me lack I do? I thought He was power over ev'rybody.

I'm growin' real fas'. Won' be long fo' I'm big enough to git a job an' leave Shetland. Wonder if God gon' help me make it happen?

I still can't believe this, but Mamma already lef' Shetland. Lef' befo' I did. She come back to see me ev'ry once in a while, but I know she ain' never comin' back to stay. I jes' been lef' in Shetland by myself with Granny.

Why you have to leave Mamma? Why didn't you want to stay here with me? Who gon'be here if I need somethin'? If Granny git sick?

Granny always tol' me Mamma went to Virginia to help Uncle Ray take care of his wife that was dyin' from the comsumpin... consumptin... or somethin' lack that. Anyhow, it's hard to remember the day she lef'. All I know is that ev'rytime she come back to see me, she always bring lotsa presents. Why once when I was real lit'l, she brought me a doll as biiig as me! An' the doll could walk, too. All I had to do was hold on to her arm real tight and she would go with me ev'rywhere. When I took a step, that doll took a big ol' stiff-legged step as big as mine if I would yank her arm.

When Mamma come back, she still the pretties' woman in the whole wide world. She real tall and skinny with the smoothes', softes', gold-color skin you could ever see. When I rub it, Mamma's face feel jes' lack Granny's brown coat. Granny say her coat is made outta somethin' call velvet. Mamma got a smile that can only be bested by her grin. When she grin, her sparkly teeth light up a big ol' light in her eyes.

I love goin' Over Town with Mamma. Ev'ry time, she come, I know we goin' at least mo' times than one. And, she gon' buy me the pretties' dresses. She buy me soxs, shoes and ribbons to match'em, too.

When I git grown, I gotta have a lotta money so I can always buy pretty dresses and shoes. I'll buy Mamma and Granny and maybe Cousin Sissy some, too. I know I have to leave Shetland to have that much money. God know it, too.

Maybe I need to git out my piggy bank now and buy somethin' to make Cousin Sissy feel better. She done lost her smile, here lately. She act pretty much lack she don' want to talk to nobody since she started stayin' at the Grace house keepin' they ugly, crazy kids. One time I didn' see her for a whole week. Granny said Miss Grace's mamma was real bad off and she had to stay in Completon to help her daddy out. But why didn't Mr. Grace stay and give his wife a hand? I saw him Over Town.

Mamma and me was Over Town one day and that was the time I firs' met my friend, Jane. Well, I don' know if I should call her my friend, her bein' White and all.

Jane's mamma and my mamma had knowed each other since they was lit'l lack me and Jane. I know this 'cause I heard'em talkin' that firs' day. I didn' hear much else, 'cause Jane an' me started lookin' at each other, smilin' and wavin' from behind our mamma's legs. Somehow even though we was real little, we knew not to let nobody see us wavin' and havin' a good time together.

All while our mamma's had they talk, Jane and me had secret talk goin' on, mos'ly with our eyes, lips and fingers. Befo' we knew anything, our mammas grabbed our hands an' pulled us down the street. We turnt our heads backwards to say "Bye" with our lips. Since then, we made a secret way to see each other an' talk.

Mamma pulled me in the Company Sto' and straight over to the pretty-dresses. When I was passin' by this one place though, I really, really wanted to feel on the silky pajamas hangin' nex' to where the gowns for ladies was hangin'. I didn' thank about that much after Mamma started puttin' the dresses with all the ruffles in fronta me to see if they look pretty. I was real glad when she bought the dress that made me look jes' like a princess.

I know Mamma know. She know I'm a princess. Mamma is the only one that know. She always callin' me "Princess." That's why I sent her my picture of the me-princess when I got through drawin' it.

I Jes' know if I was in Virginia livin' with Mamma, ev'rythang would be jeees' fine…not that it ain't good livin' with Granny. But, a girl's home is with her mamma ain' it? Oops! I have to remember what Miss Burnice said the other day.

"Alright Robin, you keep telling me you are a princess and asking why nobody, but your mamma and I know it. Well if you want other people to know, you'll have to talk better…more like a princess would talk."

"How I'm gon' do that, Miss Burnice?"

"Don't worry, Dear, I'll teach you. But you will have to practice what I tell you. You'll have to practice, practice every single day, every time you talk. Can you do that?"

"Yes Ma'am."

"You don't sound as if you really want to do this!"

"Yes I do Miss Burnice, ma'am! Yes Ma'am, I really, really want to. Please teach me, Miss Burnice, please! Teach me to talk pretty like you. Pleeeeese!"

I promised. So I got to practice what Miss Burnice tell me. Then maybe people will know me and want me 'roun' them. Who wouldn' want to be 'roun' somebody that sound lack a princess?

You don' know my cousin, Miss Burnice, do you? It's my big Cousin Darrel's wife. She use to live up North an' they got married an' came back down here in Shetland to live. Miss Burnice was a famous dancer in somethin' call the Cotton Club in New York City. Ain' no surprise to me. She real pretty an' talk real, real pretty, too. I have to find out what happen that made them come to Shetland, though. What famous people would want to come here? I'm gon' tell you soon as I find out.

Wonder how I can git somebody to tell me? Hummmmm.

Oh…most times, Mamma don' stay long when she come. She go back to Virginia where her job is. I miss her a lot when she be…(*it ain't when she be gone*), I mean, when she is gone. My family "tries," "try" or somethin', but they cain't ever take Mamma's place. Other than Granny, Auntee Jelma come the closest.

Miss Burnice tol' me I need to listen to the people tellin' the news an' that sanger, Mr. Johnny Mathis when they talk. She say they talk real good and proper. I have to tell Cousin Sissy to listen, too, whenever the next time I see her. I can ask Auntee Jelma to help. Maybe if she help me befo' Friday night prayer meetin', I can practice talkin' when I read the Bible verses to the saints. Wonder what they gon' say 'bout that?

God, you gotta help me, too! Right?

"Roe-Roe…Roe-Roe! Roe-Roe Beannie!"

"Yes Ma'am!"

"Supper is ready!"

"Yes Ma'am, I'm comin' ra't (Ooops), right now Granny."

I'm gon' talk to you some mo' when I git in the bed. I <u>can</u> talk to you somewhere else than in this tree, cain't I?

► ▼ ◄ ▲

Auntee Jelma, Uncle Ray's second wife, got the same name as his firs' wife that died. Kinda funny that all the women with all the different names, he had to marry two women with the same name. It's kinda spooky, if you ask me. After the firs' Aunteee Jelma died, Uncle Ray had come back to Shetland an' went way down to Pego and fount the second Auntee Jelma.

I don't know 'bout the firs' Auntee Jelma, but the second one is my favorite. She is real pretty. She got long, good hair. You can tell she got some White people's blood in her though, 'cause she would have to have a lotta sun befo' she would really be dark lack a Negro. Auntee Jelma is all mellow, warm and cozy whether she got on her church gloves and hat or not. She real, real healthy, too.

I love the way Auntee Jelma laugh. Her laugh come from way down inside her belly. Prob'ly start real lit'l from her funny bone an' go all the way through her belly befo' it come out her mouth. When she laugh, it always make me feel happy and glad to be where I am.

If Auntee Jelma hit her "funny bone" accident'ly, would it hurt lack mine do when I hit it? Hummmm, maybe one day I'll make that accident happen an' see.

"Oh, Lord you gotta forgive me for thankin' such a thought. I would never bring no harm to nobody. Forgive me…pleeeease!"

I cain' make nothin' happen to Auntee Jelma ra't (oops!) right now, even if I wanted to, lack you know I don't.

I have to remember and practice!

Auntee Jelma tol' me a secret she didn' even tell Granny, yet. I ain' tol', nooooo, I only tol' it to my dolly and Jane when I was in the bed playin' with them in my mind last night. At night, I have to play with my dolly in my mind, 'cause somebody stole her when I was on the train goin' to see Mamma. I have to play with Jane in my mind, 'cause Jane can't come to my house to play and I cain't go to her's. Cousin Sissy had tol' me that in Shetland, "the Negro children and White children jes' can't play together." I already knew that, but I had to ask anyway jes' 'cause I want to reeeally know.

Why not, Cousin Sissy?

"That's jes' the way it is."

I would love to tell you Auntee Jelma's secret, but you might tell. Oh that's right, you didn' tell 'bout the dam, Cousin Sissy stealin' and Grandfather, did you?

Okay, Sh-sh-sh-sh! Listen. Auntee Jelma gon' have me a l-i-t-t-l-e cousin.

Got to remember how Miss Burnice say "little," so I don' say lit'l no more. She said ev'ry time I want to say "I'm gon," put "I will" in place of it. I'm gon', no, no...I will really, really listen to ev'ry word I say from now on.

When Auntee Jelma tol' me her secret, I made her a promise that I would go git her some white dirt as many times as she wanted me to. I want her to have a big ol', healthy baby.

I don' have to go far to git white dirt. Don' have to go by myself, neither. Jes' follow the ol' folks who go git it all the time from the hilltop on the road to Over Town. Folks eat that stuff lack (Oops!), like it is candy or somethin'. You can always tell the ones who eat it a whole lot, 'cause they walk 'round with white on they (Oops!), their lips.

The other week, Miss Burnice gave me the what for. She said "It's' their,' not 'they'! Roe Roe, say 'of,' not 'uh!' And for goodness sake, please say 'more,' and not 'mo'! Every day she keep on telling' me stuff to practice. Then she talk to me a real long time so she can make sure I can say it right."

So I been tryin' to practice this stuff real hard,' cause I promise. 'Specially sayin' "like" 'steada "lack." That is real, real hard to do.

Anyhow…A few of them white dirt eaters got a little drool of white slidin' outta they (Oops!)…out of their mouth, 'til it run over their chin an' put speckle drops on their clothes that look like "pokie dots, pochie dots,"….or whatever they call. Shucks!

Or "whatever their call?" No, I think I need to say, " whatever they are called." I hope that's right.

When I firs' ate white dirt, it had a taste kind of like flour and sugar mixed up together, then some of the water took out so it was moooore like the chalk teachers write on the blackboard with. *(Wow, I said it!)* I hear all the time how white dirt is good for you, but I know I won' ever eat it like Auntee Jelma do. I would be scared I might have one of them white trickles an' not know it. I know ev'rybody would be snigglin' at me under they-rrrr breath.

How would a princess look walkin' 'round with white stuff on her lips and her dress? Some might get stuck in my ruffles.

Know what? My new little cousin gon' be sooooo lucky to have Auntee Jelma for a mamma. *(Forgot, I should have said, "will be.")* I know, 'cause when I'm with her, she make me feel almos' like her child.

If I was Auntee Jelma's real child, then maybe I could stay in Shetland.

Though I reeealy can't see it ra't (Oops!), right now, I hope Uncle Ray will be a real good daddy. I want my new little cousin to have a good mamma…and daddy.

This is somethin' else 'bout Uncle Ray. Since he move back to Shetland, I have tried and tried to figger out why all the women think he is "soooo good lookin'." I heard'em say it. But I jes' don' see it. He is a "ugly cuss" like Granny would say. Uncle Ray is black as coal and look like a whole can of Vienna sausages been smushed and rolled up together to make each one of his big ol' thick lips. His eyes ain' right, neither! (Oops!) His eyes are not right, either. *(I am talkin' 'bout more than one eye, so I have to say "are," not "is.".)* When he look at you, one eye go one way and the other stay straight. I heard somebody say Uncle Ray got hit in the eye in the war.

Am I s'pose to feel sorry for him? He make me sick. I have to pray real hard for God to change Uncle Ray's wicked ways so he can be a good daddy.

Miss Burnice will really be proud of how much I have been practicin' since she been gone. She comin' back in two days, so I can't stop. Do I really care if I never be a real princess? Naw, I jes' like talkin' better. Talkin' better make me sound more like I'm older than eleven years old. Today I will practice "think" for "thank" an' surprise her.

Okay, Uncle Ray is tall and slim an' got a voice like you hear on the radio.

Wait! That must be it! The women hear Uncle Ray's voice and th-th-ink about the radio man!

Ummmmmph!

All I know is that when I see women talkin' to Uncle Ray, their voice git, *Naaaaaw, I'm s'pose to say "get" like it rhymes with "wet."* The women's voice get all mellow and stuff. Their eyes be hard to stop dancin' 'round. Maybe that's why they have to bat'em a lot, huh? To stop them from dancin'? A big silly grin come on ev'ry one of their faces, too.

Uncle Ray's face change like that when he talkin' to Miss Rosie. I think he forget 'bout Auntee Jelma for a time.

How can you forget you a husband and daddy? Maybe bein' a husband and daddy don' mean much, huh? Maybe that's why Grandfather lef' Granny with his girlfriend and why my daddy...jes' lef'. When I get grown, my children will have the bes' home! I'll be the bes' mamma and get them the very bes' daddy, ever.

▼ ◄ ▲ ►

I remember the firs' day I saw my father. Granny woke me up early.

"Roe baby, you need to wake up so you kin dress up special today. Yo' daddy comin' to pick you up."

Jes' like that. He ain't, oops, he was not comin' to see me, but comin' to pick me up.

While I was gettin' dressed and even when Granny was combin' and braidin' my hair, I wonderd, *Who is this daddyman?* I had heard people say he lived up North. But, I hadn' ever seen him.

Waitin' for him to come, I shut my eyes real tight and tried to see my father in my head. I could see this tall handsome man with a warm sparkly smile to match Mamma's. He is all dressed up in a pretty suit bought in one of those clothes-magazine stores.

Noooooo. He gon' step outta his chariot wearin' a maganisient silky robe lack the kings in the Bible pictures. He gon' walk over, bend down, scoop me up an' carry me far, far 'way to his castle, my real home.

I knew all that was somethin' made up in my head, when I looked up and saw this strange-lookin', short, bow-legged, light-skin man standin' in the door. Granny said he was my daddy... my father... or whoever. (*Miss Burnice said to call him "Father."*) Anyhow, I took Granny's word. What else could I do?

Would Granny ever tell me a fib? Naaaw, you crazy? She saved and sanctified. You know better.

After he talked to Granny a little, my father held out his hand and said, "Well come on young lady, let's go." I took his hand, 'cause I knew Granny would whip me if I sassed. But some kind of fire start burnin' in my head that kep' me from thinkin' thoughts.

Why he keep on starin' and grinnin' at you, I thought while we was ridin' in his car. After a while, my father started lookin' like the wolf grinnin' at Lit'l Red Ridin'hood. I got real scared.

No matter where we went that whole day, my father jes' looked at me grinnin'. We went from house to house where he had other folks look at me and grin too. Sometime they said things, but I was so full of scaredness, thinkin' any minute they would grab me for harm. Scaredness kep' me from hearin' them real clear. I was a happy girl when I got back to Granny's house. I knew wherever my home, it was not with him.

He wasn't even a prince, much less a king. Wonder why he keep comin' back here every year? Why he always come pick me up? We always do the same thing: grin, grin from house to house.

"That's it! I know! He is made to come! Grandma Lettie make him come!"

Ev'ry year, my father have to drive Grandma Lettie back home for the family reunion. She prob'ly make him come get me. I can jes' hear her:

"Boy, go git that gal. I want to see my grandbaby." (*I can say "git" now, 'cause that's what Grandma Lettie say.*)

I can jes' see my father frownin', slingin' his fists from side to side, stumpin' his foot, yellin', "Ah Mamma Lettie." After he finish slingin' and stumpin', he get in the car and come get me, 'cause he know he have to do what Grandma Lettie say.

What would I do if I didn' have Miss Burnice to keep tellin' me how I need to talk? I was sho' glad (Ooops!). I was very glad when Cousin Shudda came back home with his pretty wife. I love hearin' 'bout when she was dancin' in the Cotton Club before she got hurt and couldn't anymore.

Hey, you got to wait a minute. I'm gettin' cold. Got to go in the house and get a sweater.

Be right back.

Hummmmmmm, cold weather. Let's see. It's what day of the month? Hallelujah! I get to go to school nex' Monday.

▲ ◄ ▼ ►

School is the bes'. Other than bein' in the chinaberry tree, the firs' place I ever felt safe and good was in school. I knew I would read, play and learn all kinds of stuff all day long. That made me feel real good.

The firs' day I ever started to school, I thought a lot 'bout Jane. I thought how good it would be if she could come to my school. Then, we could have lots of fun. I was wonderin' what she was thinkin' 'bout. Next time I saw her Over Town, she said she thought the same thing her firs' day, too.

Wonder if Jane and me will ever get to be the good friends we are? Whoever thought up this color thing, anyhow? When I get grown, I will find out.

A real happy time in school was when I firs' got to use numbers. I always feel real easy with numbers. Granny say, I got a gift.

When we did arithmetic problems in Miss Reed's room, she'd say, "Just check it yourself, Dears, Just check it yourself." I got so good at checkin', 'til I got to help Miss Reed check some of the others' papers. I got real good 'cause I found out if I would check my problems myself, I could know if I was right or wrong all by myself. Didn' even need to ask Cousin Sissy.

It's always been real strange how the right answers to problems jes' click in my head. Almos' as soon as I look at a problem, "click," there's a picture of the answer. And it's always the right one, too.

Why the others get problems wrong, I wonder? Granny say God gave me a gift when he gave me my clicker. She act like havin' a clicker is a real good thing. If God give clickers for presents, why don't the others have one that they can use like me? Is God a respect-a-person, or somethin'?

When I was the only one in class who got the answer right, I felt all the eyes starin' at my back. It's a real strange feeling. For a while now, school is gettin' to be like ev'ry place else in Shetland, a place where I'm odd man out. I always know the answer as soon as the teacher ask, but I don' raise my hand like I used to.

I knew the others would talk about me behind my back. Prob'ly always say I'm bein' the teacher's pet. They would pick fights with me on the way to the bus, too. When it got too hard to hold the answer behind my lips and it jes' would pop out, I got all hot inside. Wish I could disappear down through my seat, through the floor and on through the ground.

I remember when I thought, *Maybe if I pray 'bout it every night, then my lips will get stronger. That way, they would hold the answers in real good, all the time.*

Guess what? Back then when I started prayin' for help with my lips and my clicker, I jes' got to be a seven year ol' girl with a clicker for letters, too.

If the teacher called on me to read, "click," a picture of the right way to say every word would pop in my head and fly right out my mouth. I tried and tried, but still haven't found a way to keep from usin' my letter clicker. Mrs. Mitchell call on me to read in class all the time. I can't disobey her and let Granny and the devil get me. So now sometime I act like I'm having a hard time. When I do, the others sniggle under their breath like my cousins do about Mr. BD.

When I use my number and letter clickers on tests that I write, it always make the teachers smile. Seein' their smiles make me feel a little warm and good, but when they hand back my "A" papers, I tuck them away in a hurry.

I really, really hate it when everybody in the whole school go to assembly and the principal give awards. I always win one for readin', writin', spellin' and arithmetic. Granny see to it that I win one for attendance, too. She get me to that bus ev'ry single day and Cousin Wilbur drop me right at the school door.

As soon as I hear my name called, I get real hot inside and it take all my strength to get out of my seat and walk to the stage pass Lola an' Ricky. They always want to win, so they look at me like they mad or somethin'. One time,

Ricky even balled up his fist and hit me on the back of my leg when I was walkin' by him. I acted like I didn' feel nothin'. Knew if I would yell loud as it hurt, he would get in some trouble. Then as soon as we got out of school, he would pick a fight so he could beat me up.

I need some help! Can you help me find some way to keep my clickers from workin'? At least help me find where a girl with clickers can go live and be alright!

I know You gave them to me God and I ain't tryin' to be ungrateful, but if I keep on usin'em, everybody will hate me. If I stop, Granny will be mad. I am in trouble no matter what I do.

Okay, I will stop thinkin' 'bout this for now.

Know what else I do that make the teachers real proud of me? A zillion back flips in a row. And, "sing like a bird." That's what Auntee Jelma tells me ev'ry time I sing for her.

"Roe-Roe, there mus' be some magic in that Chinaberry tree, 'cause you sing jes' like them birds I see up there."

I don't get to sit in the tree much now. Granny an' school keep me real, real busy.

Know what? I don't feel hot inside when I'm tumblin' and singin'. Jes' feel warm and mellow, knowin' I am makin' ev'rybody happy. I can tell by them clappin'.

Wait a minute! Miss Burnice told me the other day that I had to start practicin' makin' my be-gin-nings and end-ings on words.

Robin, Dear, it's not "hearin' and clappin'," it's hear-ing and clap-ping. Not "'bout and 'though." Say, aaaa-bout and alllll-though. Another thing, you will have to make a sound for the "s" at the end of words, too. Sometimes you'll need to say "zzzz" and sometime "sssss". How else can the person listening tell if you are talking about more than one or if what you are talking about belongs to somebody?"

Yes Ma'am. I'll practice.

Aaaaa-bout. Claaap-ping. Alllll-though.... He has two top-ssss, five wormzzzz.... It is Mike'sss ball.

Anyhow, what people do when I tumble and sing let me know they are happy aaabout who I am. Roe-Roe, the good tumbler and good singer.

The teacher-zzzz (That's more than one. You hear it?). The teachers want to take me places with them, sometime, sometimes...or something. *(I have to ask.)* Granny let Mrs. Vines take me to Academic Showdowns where I really have to use my clickers.

I really like go-ing to sing with Mrs. Evan the bes-ttt, though. When I'm done sing-ing, she always take me to her house. She got a great big ol' television. Granny's and mine is little. Her picture ain't (oops!). Her picture isn't always as clear as Granny's, but even when it look like it's rain-ing real hard on Mrs. Evan's TV screen, I can still see Soupy and Clarabell move around. Mrs. Evans don't cut the television off when the dancing start like Granny do...does, either.

I will have to remember that if I am talking about one thing, what it is doing have to have "sss" at the end of the word...No "zzz." Miss Burnice need to tell me that again.

Maybe God didn't make dancing a wrong thing to do for Mrs. Evan. He does different kinds of things for different people, you know..

When May Day come, *(comes...No, let me see...It comes')*, the coach takes me to run races (I am real fast!) and to play in the basketball tournamen-t-t. (I am real good at playing basketball, too.) But, I enjoy it best when they pick me to plait the Maypole. Me and the others take our crepe paper strips and make sure they go under and over each other's real nice. We don't stop walkin'-ing to Mr.

Bethoven's music until that pole is all wrapped up in beautiful colors all the way down to the bottom and looking real pretty.

"Roe-Roe! Roe-Roe Beannie!"

"Yes Ma'am!"

"You come down outta that tree and go git me some 'light bread' fo' the sto' close."

"Yes Ma'am!"

Sorry. Got to go. Well…maybe that's good. I can talk to you on the way. I think I'll ride my bicycle. That way, nobody will stop and offer to give me a ride, not even the White boys that like to tease me so much. They don't talk kind like Jane. Wonder what they think I did to them?

Okay now, you know I do flips when halftime comes during the boy's basketball games, right? Jane is the only one I know who can do flips good as me. *(Alright I should say, "as good as I can," okay?)* I try extra hard when I flip during the games at the armory 'cause… beeecause I know she is watching.

Jane's daddy comes to open the armory doors and see after things when there's a game. Jane always come with him. We sit apart to watch the first half. But jes' after I get through doing flips at half-time, Jane act like she has to use it. She knows that's where I'm heading soon as I finish flipping. That way, we can sneak and talk a while. We talk mos'ly about flipping. But sometimes we pull up chairs to the corner of the hall back by the restroom door and talk about eeeeeverything.

Jane knows all kinds of things that Cousin Sissy don't….doesn't, or whatever. Anyway, Jane knows more stuff. Once, she told me about how it is in Florida. Her family go…goes *("Family" is one so it must be "goes.")* there on vacation and sit on the beach in something called a "cabana." I asked Granny about when we could go on a vacation in Florida and sit in a cabana, but she said that was for White folks.

Now what difference it make-ssssss what color you are when you're jes' sunning, swimming and sitting? Jes' because you already have color, does not mean you can't have any fun in the sun...do it, noooo, does it? Somewhere, it must be fine for folks like me to enjoy sun and water.

I know Miss Burnice told me not to say "jes." But, "just" jes' don't sound right at all.

The last time Jane and I talked, we was, nooo...were sitting in the corner by the restroom. She told me how much she had missed me the time I had had a cold and couldn't do flips at the game. That made me feel real good. Then she asked me a scary question.

"Hey Robin. Guess what. When I get real big, I'm going to run off and be a movie star! Wanna come go with me? Pleassse! That way, we could really be friends."

"May-be."

I am sooooo glad Jane never calls me Roe-Roe! 'Specially, Roe-Roe Beannie.

Ev'ry time Jane said, "Ah come on and go Robin, we can have soooo much fun," lots of butterflies would start flapping their wings in my stomach real fast. I always said maybe I would, but I knew I wouldn't. Jane would be so excited that I was scared if I said, "No, I can't" she would stop coming to watch me do flips. Would stop showin' me the ways her teacher at the White school taught her to do flips. Maybe even stop being my friend.

Sitting and having so much fun, Jane and I both forgot to watch the time. When we looked up, Jane's father was rushing for us. He looked like he wanted to do us harm. Then, he straightened his face a little, walked over and grabbed Jane with one hand and her chair with the other. He drug Jane away leaving me jes' sitting there with my mouth wide open.

When I went back in to watch the game, I looked up and saw Jane's father holding her real close by her arm. We jes' peeped at each other, smiled and when it was safe, gave our secret wave, making sure her father didn't see.

I never saw Jane again after that night. I heard the ol' folks say her father had sent her to some other school. Wish I could talk to her and find out.

Maybe Jane and I should have thought more about what people in Shetland say about color. Maybe, we should've run off together.

There was only one time when Jane and I didn't get together and talk at a game. That's the time I hid from her. This is what happened:

Granny had bought me a new outfit for flipping during the tournament. Our school colors are crimson and white, so she bought me this pretty crimson, corduroy skirt with white shorts made out of taffeta. It had a white sweater with a crimson poodle dog on the front.

At halftime, I couldn't hardly wait for the team to get off the floor so I could start flipping. I wondered why people weren't clapping and cheering the way they usually did. When I reached the other end of the court, I found out.

Mrs. Lee, the assistant principal, grabbed hold of me before my feet could hit the floor outside the court. I couldn't imagine what was wrong, but whatever it was, I figured it could wait until I finished doing my flips. When Mrs. Lee said, "Come with me dear," I told her that too.

"But I have to go back down the court. I have to finish doing my flips!"

Mrs. Lee just grabbed my arm, pulled me over to the side and whispered, "I think you have some red in your shorts down below. You may not want to do any more flips tonight, Robin."

Can you imagine how I felt? The whole armory was full and everybody knew it was my "time of the month." I thought I would die. I was hoping the floor would just swallow me up...whole.

Somehow I made it to the restroom, washed up and changed my clothes. When Jane came in, I said "Hi" real quick, ran out the door and went hid at the back of the bleachers. I jes' couldn't go out front where I knew Jane and the others would see me. Before the game was over, I ran and got on the bus. Went way to the back and sat down in the last seat in the corner, hoping nobody would try to talk to me on the way home. If I could talk to Jane now, I wouldn't care.

Granny said that God helped me to live through that night. He also helped that to be the last time I tumbled down court at halftime. Since those stains never completely left my shorts, He helped that outfit to hang in the closet in Granny's and my bedroom. Everytime I touch it accident'ly, I get all hot inside.

School has never been the same since that night. Though everybody looked all normal and stuff, I know they are laughing at me way down. That's why I don't have anything to do with any of them, if I can help it. Mostly, keep to myself. In class, my number and letter clickers finally have started to have heavy rain like Mrs. Evan's TV, so I jes' keep as quiet as I can. The only thing I do is eeeev'ry once in a while, play baseball. I think they choose me jes' because I can hit homeruns.

"Roe-Roe, you must be a tomboy, 'cause you sho' love to climb trees and play ball," Granny say.

But, sitting in the limb-arms of this big ol' Chinaberry tree talking to you, is the <u>only</u> thing that make me feel safe and good, now. It certainly is the only time I can look far, far away. I hope that I am close enough to God so maybe one day He will let me see where I need to go.

Ouch!   Ouch! Ouch!

PART II

ROBIN

▼◄▲►

"*Ouch, ouch, ouch!*" *Nobody ever told me it would hurt like this. I will jes' have to fold my arms and hold them real, real tight. I can't stop running now.*

"Johnny Ray, you better git outta my way with your fat self, or I'll run right on top of you,"

I'm gonna make this homerun, I don't care what happen, or how many people see my face all scrunched up from hurt."

It had never hurt that bad before. I knew I had to tell Granny, but I was scared.

That's why I am so glad I have you to talk to, especially about girl things. I hardly ever see Cousin Sissy anymore. When I do, she jes' look at me strange, hug me real tight and tell me, "Roe-Roe, you always try to be a good girl, you hear." No matter how many times I ask her where she been and when will I see her again, she jes' says the same thing. Nothing else. I tried to tell her about the knots, but she jes' got a faraway look in her eyes like she wasn't hearing me.

It's been a while ago since I felt these little knots in my chest. Thought I had caught some kind of disease.

Oh Lord, what's this happening to me? Please don't let me die! What You want me to do? Okay, I promise I will never think gossip about the saints. Please don't let me die! I'm too young! Ain't, (Shucks!), haven't been any place, but Shetland and Virginia, yet! I have to go see New York City where Miss Burnice used to be famous. Gotta go over in Africa with the kings and queens jes' once. Since this kind of stuff happens to people over there all the time, they might have some medicine for it.

I had seen on the tv how people over in Africa had knots jes' grow up on their body for no reason. Sometimes it killed'em, too.

Wonder how that happens. Wonder why, since they live in "God's paradise." That's what I always hear my pal's real ol' grandma say all the time.

"My home place, Africa? Well ya jes' talkin' 'bout God's Sweet Paradise. Chil'uns, dere's where duh, trees jes' be filled up wid bananas an' papya, jes' ripe an' hangin' ready fuh duh pickin'."

Then she got this song she always sing:

Home sweet home!

Oooh home sweet home!

God's sweet paradise Africa

My home sweet home!

Every time I thought about Miss Dote's singing, I saw myself in Africa bowing before the king for a royal cure.

The knots grew real fast. They got real big and heavy, too. Started bouncing up and down real hard all the time and bringing pain to my chest like you wouldn't believe!

When I run bases is the worst. Shoot, they hurt a lot when I jump rope, too.

I knew I had to tell Granny as soon as I got home that day. She would have to give me a pill or rub me with her special salve…or something.

You would never guess what Granny did when I told her. She jes' laughed a little under her breath and said, "We gotta go Over Town and buy you some brazeeahs." Then she laughed another funny little laugh that went into a smile that looked like the plaster man had put there on his real, real happy day.

Is Granny laughing at me, too?

I was flavagasted. I thought Granny would put her arms around me, lead me to the kitchen and give me something to make the pain go away. But did she? Naaaw! Granny jes' sat a spell, grinning. I didn't know what to do.

Should I go to bed? Naaaw, it's still daytime. Should I go outside to the tree? Naaaaw, if I run out now, Granny'll think I'm disrespecting.

Like the frozen block of ice the iceman used to put in the icebox when I was real little, I jes' stood there looking at grinning Granny with heat taking over my whole body. The heat must have made the ice melt, because soon heavy rain was covering up my mind. When I knew anything, Granny had gone out the room. I didn't even remember her getting out of the chair. A paper strip like what they put the movie shows on started winding through the rainshower in my mind. The strip was white with black writing, but didn't make that flapping noise like in the show when the movie ends.

"Don't nobody really care how you feel," I read on the paper while it circled around and around in a smooth wave. "You got to find a way to get out of here so people can't make fun of you. You have got to find a way to get...." I read it over and over for I don't know how long.

When the words started fading away, I remembered how when I had heard the big girls in the restroom say, "I sho' am glad I got this bra to hol'up my titties, 'specially when I'm jumpin' rope and runnin'....." As soon as they saw me, they stopped talking and snatched their blouses down real fast like.

Do they think I don't know they're showing each other? They must think I am stupid.

My girl classmates probably thought I was stupid, jes' because I was the youngest in my class. I was the youngest because of what Principal Rowell and the teachers did at the end of my fourth grade year.

"Robin, tell your grandmother your teachers and I have decided to move you up to the sixth grade for next year."

"Thank you Principal Rowell."

"Is that all you have to say?"

"Thank you Principal Rowell, Sir."

Who he think want to go to a higher grade so Ricky can really beat'em up, all the time?

Yea, they thought I was too stupid to know anything. Ev'ry time I went to "use it," my girl classmates acted like they had this big ol' secret they jes' had to hide. They would be staring at each other with big ol' grins waiting for me to leave.

Don't they know I hear them bust out laughing as soon as I close the door.

The same day I heard the girls talk the first time, I couldn't wait to get home. I opened up the door real fast and ran to Granny's bookshelf where she kept books for me to read about growing up and stuff. I completely forgot what I had vowed.

I ain't never gonna read that ol' nasty book with pictures of naked people in it. Don't know why Granny bought it, anyway. Didn't she see the pictures of them women's private parts?

Now Granny ain't trying to trick me to the devil, is she?

"Naaaaaaaaw silly, Granny saved!"

Oh, excuse me. That jes' slipped out.

Anyhow, I turnt to the page where they had pictures of ladies with braziers on. Ev'ry bra looked like a contraption you wouldn't believe!

Look to me like the harness I see Uncle Ray put on ol' China. Imagine being harnessed like a horse.

I jes' knew I would have to be a grown woman before I would need something like that. Thought the girls in the restroom was jes' being fast.

How can anybody climb trees with a harness on? Already I can't climb when it's my time of the month. I have cramps too bad. Granny say in that time, I have to be a lady. But what kind of lady can you be in a harness? I don't think Granny would really want me to wear bras all day long, all the time. Would she?

I sho' would like to ask Cousin Sissy, "How can you wear a bra all day? Don't it hurt your back and shoulders?" That's what I want to ask her. But I haven't seen her in a real, real long time, now. Something's wrong. I jes' know it. Nobody ever says anything about her so I can hear.

Maybe I can find a way to see her. Maybe if I skip school and go to Mr. Grace's house... Naaaaw, Granny would kill me. Maybe if I....

Hey! Hey! Do <u>you</u> wear bra contraptions? Oh I forgot, you don't talk back. I wish I could find some way to make you. I'm smart. Maybe one day I will.

Guess what. Granny and I did go Over Town to the Company Store. We didn't only get "brazeeahs," but she bought me two girdles and got me two pieces of material, too. I was glad she got the material, because I needed to practice sewing. All I had to sew on was that ol' pedal Singer machine that's been sitting in front of the window in Granny and my bedroom ev'ry since I can remember.

I needed to practice a lot. Miss Green, my Home Economics teacher, told me so after making me undo and redo twenty zillion stitches. I took those stitches out so many times 'til the material started getting holes in it like you wouldn' believe!

"Roe-Roe, you got to get that seam straight," Miss Green always say.

Miss Green feel it alright to call me Roe-Roe, since she is Uncle Reuben's wife. I will have to straighten her out somehow. Roe-Roe is a little kid's nickname.

How do I get Miss Green to call me Robin without sassing? Maybe I can have Granny ask her not to. That way, maybe Granny will stop some of the others from calling me Roe-Roe, too.

"You can pick out any pattern you want," Granny had said as we jes' finished crossing the bridge, on our way Over Town. She had been quiet before then.

I picked out a pattern with a round scalloped neck and scallops at the end of some short sleeves. It even had scallops down at the hem. The picture of that dress on the pattern envelope was so pretty. In the car going home, I stared at the pattern so long, that I missed looking for the mill people.

"Which piece of material should I make up first?"

"What you say my grown up Roe-Roe Beannie?"

"Nothing Granny. Jes' talking to myself."

Hummmm, I know what…I'll ask Auntee Jelma. She can pick things real good.

I sewed the light yellow material first. It was my favorite. That material felt sooooo good when I brushed my hands across it. And when I rubbed it on my face, it glided across like it had been made by millions of them worms that…uuuh, you know, the worms that have strings coming out their bodies. I knew the material had come out of the cotton bow and the mill, though. I ain't (Oops!), I'm not stupid, no matter what my girl classmates think. You know I am smart. You know about my clicker gifts.

"Be careful with the scallops," Granny yelled from her chair under the Chinaberry tree where she had started sittin' every evening until it got dark.

"Yes Ma'am, I'll be careful!"

Good thing I started talking to you when I was out of the tree. I wouldn't be able to get pass Granny without sassing.

I cut and sewed the curve of every scallop real careful, so I wouldn't have to take loose not one stitch. Wanted to make sure Granny and Miss Green would be proud when I showed them what I had done.

I finished my dress jes' in time for the spelling bee and Young People's Willing Workers (YPWW) program at church. When Granny saw my dress finished, I knew I had done a good job. I didn't only see a smile on her face, but got a big ol' hug. That Saturday, she took me Over Town and bought me some leather, yellow shoes that had the toes and heels cut out and a strap that tied around my ankles in a bow. They even had, ummmmmm, maybe about a one-inch heel. She bought me some of those silk stockings I had seen in the catalog, too. They didn't have the seam down the back, though. That time we didn't go to the Company Store. We went to Raglins!

I got all dressed up for Miss Burnice when she was helping me practice for the spelling bee. She told me, "Robin, come over after school on Tuesday so I can do your hair real pretty. I'll fix it so you will look like an almost grown-up princess."

◄▲►▼

From the time I got to the spelling bee, ev'rybody kept telling me, "Roe-Roe, you sho' look good." I already knew I was looking good, but ev'ry time they said it, I felt all warm and homey inside. When time came for me to go up on the stage and spell, though, I felt like something jumped inside me and was keeping me from walking right. I could barely hear what the caller said. Or, see the judges real good. Rain started falling over my letter pictures like you wouldn't believe! The rain got real heavy like it did after the last time I flipped at half time. I never thought my being dressed up would make my letter pictures have so much rain 'til I couldn't see the word "across" clear. So I spelled it

"a-c-c-r-o-s-s."

"Robin, you may take your seat."

"Yes ma'am."

"Thank's for your participation. The next word is...."

I hadn't sat down but a minute before the rain stopped. No sooner than Miss Jackson finished saying a word, "click," there was the spelling ev'ry time. The right spelling jes' popped in my head so clear!

Sunday came and I got to wear my new outfit to YPWW. Knowing how pretty I looked, I sung my solo the best ever. After the program, everybody was suppose to go to the Gathering Hall, but I had to pee first. While I was back in the stall "using it," some saints came in. You will neeeeever guess what I heard that time.

"Ain'it a shame dat she let dat chil' weah dem stockin's and high heeahs? Look lack she got her on a gird'l, too!"

"Unnnnnn Hunnnnn, it sho' do."

I thought they were talking about Granny, again. Jes' like before, I knew so when I could see their faces.

There was no fellowshipping for me that day. I even told Veronica "no" when she asked me if I wanted to go outside with her to play. I had to look and see what other saints were talking about Granny and me behind our backs.

Wonder why the saints keep going to the restroom to talk bad? The devil must hide out in there and wait for them, or something, If this is how the saints and church will always be, I know this is not the place for me to be.

I stared at every set of moving lips so hard that I could nearly see what the saints were saying before they said it. I knew I could neeeever feel easy in that church again. But I couldn't stop going, because I had to keep close watch in case I heard something else that I needed to tell Granny. Besides, Granny would never let me stop going to church, anyway.

You think other people talk about me and Granny like the saints do? Man, I wish you could talk back to me. I want to hear what you sound like. Awfully glad, though, that I don't have to stop talking to <u>you.</u> Now listen to this.

While I was out of school for Christmas, I started sewing the other piece of material Granny bought me. I used the same scalloped pattern, but the dress looked real, real different made up in material with big ol' purple and green flowered blooms with dark blue in the background. That material had big ol' splotches of brown that made it look like some I had seen wrapped around women over in Africa when I was looking at the nature-magazine pictures at Cousin Russell's house. Those women looked so pretty like you wouldn't believe! They had all that white ivory, gold and wood that had been carved a special way hanging around their heads and necks. Don't worry, I know I couldn't ever wear all that jewelry. The saints would reeeealy talk, then.

One day, I have got to go over there for a visit! In Africa I bet I could wear whatever I want to. Maybe even get some holes ev'rywhere. Then, I could wear a ring in my nose and some great big ol' earrings. Wonder if getting them big ol' holes hurt real bad?

If I can do anything I want in Africa, maybe I will stay over there to live. Hummmmm, maybe even get married to a prince...or a king, since sometime they get to be king real young.

While I was sewing that day like I am right now, I thought a lot about being in Africa. I saw myself being one of those African princesses, all dressed up and walking through the palace followed by all the ladies that serve me. Could jes' see me and my ladies walking over to where the throne room is, to be with my mamma and daddy, the king and queen, for a little while. As soon as I walked into the room, my father would open his arms and....

Ouch, ouch my finger!

Don't you laugh! That hurt!

Anyhow, I finished my other dress and wore it to the science fair. Even Robbie Hill said I looked good, and he "kain stan' girls," he say. I know Diana and Deborah wished he could with both their hearts.

I was real proud of my science-fair project. Made oxygen from zinc and acid. There I stood in my new, best, favorite dress, but with flat shoes this time. I only looked at my yellow heels standing in the corner of my closet with the stockings tucked deep inside.

I won't wear them again, even if anybody asks me. I saw how pretty they looked on the woman in the magazine, but she don't have to be around the saints. I won't ever have people talking about Granny again if I can help it.

▶▼◀▲

"The combination of zinc and sulfuric acid produces oxygen."

I wondered if I had said it jes' the way Mrs. Vines had rehearsed me over and over and over. The judges were standing right in front of me. I couldn't mess up.

Then I said, "Allow me to demonstrate, please."

When I took the top off the flask to drop the zinc pellets inside, the acid popped out and onto the front of my dress. It was all I could do, not to say a nasty word. Don't worry…I didn't. By the time I got back to Granny's house, though, I could tell every place the acid had dropped. Four places, four holes.

Maybe I should never try to make clothes. Was it that I was too proud of my dresses? The Bible say, "Pride goest before a fall." Whatever is making the dresses I make fail, I will jes' pray that it be removed like I hear Granny do.

Hey! Did you say "good?" Ya know, sometimes it seem I can hear you.

My exhibit won second place and I was soooo happy to take my trophy back to give to Principal Rowell so he could put it in the display case in the front hall for the whole school to see. When I handed the trophy to him, I am sure I turnt blush-red like I used to see Jane and other White folks do, sometime. When he looked at me with proudness all over his face, I could have burst wide open.

The next week, Principal Rowell had a meeting with Granny. He told her how proud he was of me and offered to give me a job. For one hour and a half after school on Monday, Wednesday and Friday, I was to go to his office and file papers. That way, he could keep up with his work. He wanted me to do a little typing, too. That would help his secretary keep up with her work. He would bring me home when I was through.

"Mrs. Talbin, I am offering Robin this job because I think she will do well. She's the fastest typist in the school. Types faster than my secretary," Principal

Rowell said to Granny, while keeping his eyes looking at me. "Do you think $4.00 a day is satisfactory pay?"

Let me see how much that is…(click!). That's twelve dollars ev'ry week. That's as much as my cousins make for picking cotton two whole days. Can you imagine how many pieces of material I can buy with that much money? I could make all kindsa things! Maybe even a whirly coat like the one Mrs. Vines wears when she's real dressed up to go somewhere after school. Wow, twelve dollars every single week!

I know. I'll have to save some of it.

After the second week of my job, though, soon as I walked in the door, I told Granny I didn't want to work for Principal Rowell anymore. All she said was, "Okay Roe, you don't have to." She never asked me why and I never told her how hard it was to type, file and try to keep Principal Rowell from grabbing me at the same time.

My last day at work, I finally had to commit what I knew Reverend Steve would call the "sin of disrespecting your elders" and jes' tell that principal.

"If you try to touch me again, I will slap the damn hell out of you and tell Granny what you did."

I couldn't believe I had said that. There it was, jes' popping outta my mouth like you wouldn't believe! Auntee Jelma would think my mouth needed a good washing. But I <u>had</u> to tell him.

God, You won't throw me straight to the devil for saying "damn, will You?"

"Principal Rowell, you give me my money and take me home right now," I said.

He did.

We didn't say one word all the way home. I didn't even look at him. Kept my head turnt looking out the window. After that, I saw Principal Rowell only when

I had to. When it couldn't be helped. I was glad there was jes' one more month and a half before school would be over.

I don't know about trustin' God and His angels to protect me like Granny say. Maybe, sometime I jes' have to protect myself, especially from the likes of Principal Rowell and the saints.

◄ ▲ ► ▼

The next year when I was in the ninth grade, we got a new principal. We got Mrs. Lester. I would only see Principal Rowell on May Day. Would only see him then because our school and lots of other schools celebrated May Day where he was the new principal.

At May Day, the best thing happened to me. Let me tell you this...I met Keith Barker! He was in the eleventh grade.

Keith looked a whole lot like Auntee Jelma, Uncle Ray's second wife, but only taller with hazel colored eyes. He smiled like Mamma and walked like walking was real, real, real good to him. Once he said, "Hi I'm Keith, what's your name," we spent almost the rest of the day together.

In the morning, Keith and me (Oops!), Keith and I watched ev'ry event together (except the ones I was in and then I was glad he was watching). We ate lunch together, then, sat together in the bleachers to watch the afternoon basketball games. Between the third and last game, Keith asked if we could go out and get some fresh air.

"Sure."

While we were outside, we decided to sneak off down the hill to where the buses were parked so we could talk private. A lot of people were walking around, so we got into one of the busses and sat down. In that big yellow bus is where I got my very first kiss. Or, I prob'ly should say kisses.

Keith kissed me three times. He did that French kissing I had heard the girls whisper about in the restroom. That last kiss left my tongue and whole body all hot like you wouldn't believe! Like magic, Keith turned into a fireball and caught me on fire. I got scared. Knew it was time for me to get out of that bus before I burnt up. So I didn't say a word, jes' jumped up, ran out the bus and back up the hill. I stopped at the gym door to catch my breath and straighten up, then went inside and sat back up in the bleachers jes' as the last game started.

Near the end of the first quarter of the game, I saw Keith come through the door. I froze. He didn't come to sit beside me.

"Whew!"

I never saw Keith after that day.

Every move Keith made when he was kissing me, I have to remember. If I do like Keith did, I will be a kisser like you wouldn't believe!

If eeeever somebody say I'm a good kisser, I know I should say, "Thank you Keith Barker!"

Know what pops in my mind every time I see a boy for the first time? I think, *Wonder if he got that "Barker fire" in him*?

Do you think I will ever find it? The Barker fire, I mean. How many times? When I do, you think I'll get scared?

I can't wait to ask Cousin Sissy about this! Oh yea I forgot. Cousin Sissy went to Georgia to visit. She sure has been gone a long, long time. Wonder when she's coming back? If she's not coming back, I sure am glad she came and told me goodbye. How she sounded scared me a little, though. You are the only one I have to talk to, now.

Let me tell you something else. I don't really know why, but my titties didn't know when to stop growing. That's why they're so big, now. I heard the girls say in the restroom, "Girl, you oughtta let a boy touch'em. Then your titties grow real big."

Oh dear God, I am sorry I let Keith touch my tits! Please stop them from growing! Pleassssse!

I was fourteen and the youngest girl in my class. Was the skinniest, too, but with the biggest titties. I looked like a popsicle stick with two big ol' oranges hanging on it.

My big tits took over my face. I don't mean they grew all over my face. I jes' mean that anytime a boy talked to me, he could never look at my face for looking at them.

"Hey! Hey! Here I am up here," I always wanted to squat down and yell. For a long time now, boys have been trying to find ways to bump up against me so they can touch them. Huh, Uncle Ray, too.

Know what? I remember this one Sunday when I stayed home from church because my stomach was hurting real bad. It was my time of the month, you know. I was laying down on the couch watching TV when Uncle Ray came into the room, walked over and jes' bent down and started feeling my tits. I jumped up and ran out on the porch so fast like you wouldn't believe! I don't even remember opening the door. Jes' "zip" and I was off the couch and on the porch.

Boy did I get Uncle Ray good, though. I filled up a big bucket from the outside spout, sat on the porch and waited. When he came through the door all dressed up in his brand new gray suit with his pink shirt and pink and gray tie he had jes' bought new from Sears and Roebuck, I went into action. It made me mad, too, that he pro'bly came home to change so he could go see Miss Rosie while Auntee Jelma was still in church.

"Zip! Splash!"

"What the…what the f—k? You little bitch! I'm gon' kill you!"

I dumped the whole bucket over Uncle Ray's head, then ran real fast like a bat outta hell.

"Oops!"

Shoot, that's alright. I have to remember. "Hell" is in the Bible, lots of times. I have to do some more reading and see what other cuss words are in there, too.

When I looked back and saw Uncle Ray trying to shake the water off, I knew he would prob'ly, really kill me if he could catch me. He tried, but remember, I run track.

"Lecher." That's what I used to hear Cousin Sissy call Uncle Ray. Wondered if there was such word. Granny's dictionary say it is, but I never hear anybody else say it.

When I ran from Uncle Ray, I didn't go back home 'til I saw Granny and Auntee Jelma come back from church. Uncle Ray had left long before that. I jes' sat in the yard at Cousin Sissy's house and talked to my other cousins. I didn't mention what had happened though. I was scared they might tell and it would be a big ol' family mess.

I was scared that Uncle Ray might sneak into the room and kill me while I was asleep, so I thought I better tell Granny.

"Don't take anymore presents from him, Roe," Granny said in a voice so low I could hardly hear.

"Don't take anymore presents from him?" Is that what Granny said? Maybe she didn't hear me.

I started telling Granny again. She stopped my telling and said the same thing again with the same look on her face I had seen that day Uncle Ray was telling her things about Grandfather.

Could it be she really did hear what I said? She heard me say Uncle Ray was touching me where he shouldn't and did not one thing about it? The only presents I get from him are ones for getting all "A"s on my report card. How can

Granny not at least <u>say</u> something to Uncle Ray? If this was my house, I would put him out. Ain't that what a Granny should do?

Granny's look let me know not to say any more. But in my head, I had another squall of rain and a fireball in my gut. I jes' knew two things: One was I would always have to keep one eye opened to watch for Uncle Ray all the time. The other one was that I had to keep something nearby me to get him with if he tried something, again.

The next time Uncle Ray try to touch me, he will be real sorry! I'm going to get one of those knives from the kitchen drawer and keep it under my mattress. If he bother me again, I'll hurt him real bad like what happened to Grandfather.

But what if Uncle Ray take the knife from me and kill me? Oh God, what should I do? If I can't tell Granny, I can't tell nobody! What can I do?

▲ ▶ ▼ ◀

After always having to scheme how to keep out of Uncle Ray's sight, I was a happy soul when I read the letter from Grandma Lettie. She wanted Granny to pack me up and send me to live with her up North for a while. Although I didn't want to leave Granny, Auntee Jelma and my two little cousins, it was my chance to get away from the likes of Uncle Ray. I begged and begged like you wouldn't believe. Finally after school was out, Granny said, "yes."

Maybe up North is where I'm suppose to be, anyhow.

The day came when I stepped on the Humingbird train with the lady from Traveler's Aide. Granny, Auntee Jelma and I had hugged goodbye in the station. They couldn't come on the train with me.

"It is our policy that family members not board the train. It's better for the children that way. "

The Aide lady's voice went real high up and she had the same smirky-like look on her face I had seen on Miss.Grace's face when she talked to Cousin Sissy and Auntee Vee. Her nose and lips turnt up like talking to them was a real nasty thing.

The Aide lady could be some kin to Miss Grace and the doctors and nurses at the Shetland hospital. They all have that same look. Lips turnt up. I hope I never have to go to that hospital. Hope I never get sick in Shetland at all.

On the train, the Aide lady gave me some papers to give to the Aide people up North. Then, she said something to this real good-looking Negro porter and left. He looked at me and smiled one of those "Barker" smiles. I smiled back, feeling all warm inside.

I really didn't think that an almost 15 year old needed traveling aide, but Granny wouldn't have it any other way. It wasn't bad though, since there were two of us and the other was only ten. She was White, so I pretended I was taking her on the trip for her folks. That way, people would think I was more grown up.

Jessica and I had a real good time together. When we got off the train and her mamma and daddy finished hugging her, she asked if I could come home with them. They said, "Sure, that would be lovely Dear," prob'ly because they knew I couldn't. I looked and saw Grandma Lettie coming toward us.

After Grandma Lettie hugged me, she turned to Jessica's folks and said, "Good afternoon Dr. Hamilton. Miss Hamilton."

"How are you Lettie," Miss Hamilton said. "Is this your granddaughter?"

"Yes, it is."

"This is my granddaughter, Jessica." Raymond's daughter."

Wonder how they know each other? I'll ask Grandma Lettie tomorrow.

We rode to Grandma Lettie's house in one of those "taxicab" cars. I was surprised to find out that riding in a taxicab was jes' like riding in the back seat of Uncle James' Chevy. When I saw a taxi on TV, I thought the ride would be something special.

"Where you live, Grandma Lettie?"

"I live in a four-family flat on 14th street, Robin."

"Oh."

Glad she didn't call me Roe Roe.

When we got there, the four-family flat building looked jes' like a big ol' house where a lot of people lived. It was jes' like with Granny and me sharing with Uncle Ray and his family, only each one of the families had their own door they could lock. We didn't.

The outside of the building looked kind of dark and dreary, but then Grandma Lettie unlocked the door to number two and we walked into the light of her living room. What you see in ev'ry other livingroom was there: A couch with a coffee table in front. There was two chairs and two end tables, one sitting between the couch and one of the chairs and the other, next to the other chair that was in the corner facing the couch. But I had only seen furniture that pretty in White folk's houses and magazines.

All Grandma Lettie's livingroom furniture was mos'ly white. The chairs were covered with some kind of silky material with teeny, tiny light blue flowers every once in a while. They had sinkholes all over the back of them with little buttons hid inside. The couch was like that too, but it was all white and had white wood carved with gold twirls that looked kind of like a grape vine all the way around the edges. The chairs jes' had the wood coming down the arms. The table legs were made from the same twirly wood with thick pieces of marble on the tops. Silvery blue rug material covered the whole floor so you couldn't see any of it, not even a little bit.

The white smokey glass lamps (one on each of the end tables) had real, light blue shades, trimmed in white rows of silky, scrunched-up braids. Little pieces of clear glass that had been cut to look like teardrops hung all the way around the bottoms of each one of them. The lamps looked like some I had seen in the magazine. Looked like they were from a castle over in England.

There were some real pretty pictures on three of Grandma Lettie's walls. The one at the back of the couch though, looked strange. It was a picture of a big steamboat that had what looked like teeny-tiny, clear Christmas tree lightbulbs sticking through teeny-tiny holes. You could only see the ends of the bulbs, but I know a Christmas tree bulb when I see one.

Why would a picture with Christmas tree lights be hanging on Grandma Lettie's wall in July? Don't she know Christmas was last year in December?

Grandma Lettie was standing, looking at me and smiling. All of a sudden, she jes' walked over to the couch, bent over and plugged the picture cord into the socket. When the picture lit up, the lights flashed on and off in the water part, making it look like it was moving. At the back of the boat, the lights went on and off in the big paddle part, too. That made it look like the paddle was turning round and round. Made it seem like the boat was really moving. The picture made me think about the times I went fishing way up the Shetland river. Didn't make me homesick enough to want to go back, though. See, every time I went with somebody boat-fishing, it was with Uncle Ray. No siree, I wanted to stay right there with Grandma Lettie.

Granny had told me that Grandma Lettie and her sister started living together after both their husbands died. Aunt Sweetney took care of things in the house, while Grandma Lettie went to work.

When I looked around, I didn't see where in the world I would sleep, but I surmised that since Grandma Lettie had sent for me, she had it figured out. I jes' stopped concerning myself and washed up and went to the table when I was called.

Aunt Sweetney had cooked all of my favorites: Fried chicken, macaroni and cheese, collard greens and the best cornbread I had ever tasted. Before I tasted Aunt Sweetney's bread, I thought Auntee Jelma made the best cornbread in her pan that made each piece look like a little ear of corn.

You want to know gooooood? Take one of Auntee Jelma's little corn-ear cornbreads while it is hot, slice it open and spread some fresh-churned butter on it. When you put it back together and bite it, all you could say is, "uummmmm umm." It tastes real good like you wouldn't believe! Aunt Sweetney's bread tasted different from Auntee Jelma's. Her's tasted more like cake cornbread.

I loooove any kind of cake.

For dessert, we had "Peachberry Rapture." Aunt Sweetney told me how to make it. She said that in a baking dish, you make a bottom layer with canned, delicious peaches, then you put in a layer of crushed graham crackers. You make the next layer with "smushed" bananas, then another layer of the graham crackers. The top layer is peaches again. While you are making the layers, you have some Eaglebrand milk mixed with cranberry sauce boiling on the stove, so when you finish with all the layering, you can pour it over ev'rything. (Make sure you got enough to soak down to the bottom!) Now put the whole thing in the oven for 30 minutes at about 375 degrees.

While that's in the oven, you can whip up some egg white and a little sugar for your meringue to go on top. After the meringue is put on, you put the Peachberry Rapture in the oven again, jeeees' long enough for the top to get a pretty brown. If you want, you can make little swirls in the meringue so you get different shades of brown on top like Aunt Sweetney do.

You *talkin' about goooood! Yea man, don'cha jes' know it! That Peachberry Rapture is crumble-in-your-mouth good like you wouldn' believe! With this good eating, maybe I can stay here with Grandma Lettie and Aunt Sweetney for a long, long while. Maybe, forever. Jes' go visit Granny, Mamma, Auntee Jelma and oh, the chinaberry tree.*

After we finished eating and washing up the dishes, I thought I should help Grandma Lettie take my clothes out the suitcase and put them away. When I asked her where to put my things, you would neeeever guess what she told me.

"You're not staying with me, Robin Dear. You're going home with your daddy. In fact, he's picking you up on his way home from work."

"He what," I heard myself scream. I knew better than to sass, but I jes' couldn't help it.

The pictures in my mind started flashing so fast that they turnt fuzzy. I could hardly see one before the next one came. One thing was clear though: Granny and I had been tricked. We thought I was coming up North to live with Grandma Lettie, when all the time the plan was for me to be handed over to my father…daddy, or whoever he is.

Maybe <u>you</u> can help straighten this out in my mind: There I was, tricked, a long way from home and no way to let Granny know what happened. No money. What would you have done? I didn't even know how to get back to the train station.

What I did was jes' started praying over and over in my mind, "God You gotta really help me this time." For a long, long time, I jes' stood in the same spot. Couldn't move. When I could, I went and scooted up in the corner of Grandma Lettie's couch, folded my arm on the corner wood, then laid my head over on it and pretended I was sleep. I never did go to sleep. I was too scared.

If they think I'm 'sleep, I don't have to talk. I can't open my mouth. If I do, I know that strange voice will come out, the one I hear coming out my mouth sometime when I'm mad. The one that cuss. That voice always get me in trouble, so I can't let it out.

While I was laying there, I was jes' listening so when I got to talk to Granny I could tell her everything that really happened.

Before long, my father came through the door, grinning like always. When I heard him, I had sat up and opened my eyes. He hugged and kissed Aunt Sweetney and Grandma Lettie and waved in my direction. He talked with them for a little while.

"Well come on young lady, let's go."

My father was picking up my suitcase off the floor. I jes' followed him to his car like I did the first time he came to pick me up from Granny's house. Felt like I was being led off to that guillotine I had read they used in England to chop off heads back in the olden days. Prob'ly, I would have felt better than I did right then if an ax had fell on my neck and erased my mind's pictures... forever.

▲ ▶ ▼ ◀

My father's house looked dreary on the outside. The next day, it did look better in the bright sunshine, though. Inside the house was kind of pretty. It had a couch and chair in the living room with lots and lots of pillows on them in a lot of pretty colors. The door to the dining room was real wide and curved, without any door. You know how I mean. I could see the whole dining room from the living room.

This house looks like a real home. But I wonder if they jes' trying to trick me.

My father grinned big when he introduced me to his wife and my two new brothers. My father's wife had a smile almost as bright as Mamma's, but there was something not quite right in her eyes when she looked at me. When she looked at me, I felt like there was something not quite right in her thoughts about me, either.

I was real glad to have brothers, though. They were older than me, too. Jimmy was sixteen and Royce, seventeen. Glad to finally have somebody I knew would look out for me and protect me, though neither one of them was my whole brother. Only one was even my half. The youngest one.

There were only two bedrooms in the house. My brothers had twin beds in one and the other was for my father and his wife. I had to sleep on the cot in the dining room. That was alright, except on the nights when my father and his pals came home in the middle of the night and woke me up talking all loud and slurry.

Didn't get much sleep that first night. Thought a lot about what I should call everybody. There was no way I could call my father and his wife "Mom" and "Dad" the way my brothers did.

I know, I can jes' call them by their names! Noooo, Granny would call that "disrespectin'." The Bible say you have to "honor thy mother and father." I sure don't want to cut my days short. Oh God, help me to be alright in this place?

For some days, I jes' kept very quiet and looked at everything and everybody a lot. I only spoke when I had to and I watched a lot of TV. Oh,…if my father and his wife told me to do something, I did it right away. I knew that's what Granny would want me to do.

For you, Granny, I will be the perfect young lady. I will make you proud!

It wasn't long before I had my routine "down pat." I knew when to talk and when to be quiet, when to move and when to stay still. I did what I needed to do and waited and waited and waited.

I was a happy soul when it was finally time for school to start. I was tired of having rain covering my mind's pictures. The pictures had started jumping around a lot, too. Sometimes they would speed up so fast 'til I jes' got fuzz, other times, they would go so slow until it was like I was in a fog. I jes' knew that when I started school my mind would clear. I wouldn't have to watch out to see what anybody was thinking and saying anymore, because my new friends would not be saints and would not know about the last night I did flips in the armory.

► ▼ ◄ ▲

That first day of school, I got up extra early and was finished in the washroom before the others woke up. I dressed real pretty in one of my brand new outfits my father's wife had brought home for me. *(Both my father and his wife turnt out to be much better than I thought)*. I combed my hair in a real pretty style, theeeen, my father's wife said I should put on a little lipstick.

Can you believe it? She wants me to go out looking like a Jezebel woman!

I knew that if Granny had seen me with my lips red, right then she would take me in the washroom and wash it off. Then, she would pray over me for the next three days. Father's wife jes' took her lipstick, put some on my lips, rubbed her lips together and said, "Do like this!" I did what she said, but went out the door scared that any minute the devil would jump out from somewhere and grab me.

I walked to school with…no, behind my brothers. I had never seen so many people walking around at one time, except at May Day. When I chanced to look in their faces, most of them were children on their way to school like me and my bothers. I couldn't imagine so many children going to one school. I knew this was up North in the big city, but seeing the White children going in the same direction as the Negroes was scary.

They're even laughing, talking and playing together.

Well I'll be! They're hugging each other, too!

I had to think real hard to make my mouth close.

When I saw the school building, all I could do was say, "wow." It was so big like you wouldn't believe!

I know if I get lost in that building, I'd jes' be a lost child. Prob'ly would stumble around and never find my way. Nobody would ever find me.

My brothers took me straight to the office and gave me some papers to give to the principal. Jes' when they got to the office door going out, they heard the secretary.

"You are new here, aren't you? Do you have your records?"

I jes' stood there looking at her still holding the papers, prob'ly with my mouth open. How was I suppose to know I was holding records? Besides, they told me to give the papers to the principal.

My brothers stopped and looked at each other in a way that made me feel they were talking about me in code, like they did sometime. Royce rolled his eyes up to the sky, sucked his teeth at the same time, then walked over and snatched the papers out of my hands. When he walked towards the counter to give the secretary my records, I walked up behind him.

"Will you go over there and sit until they call your name," Royce shouted at me with his face all frowned up. He was talking at me, but looking at Jimmy. They left the office in a big hurry, not even looking back to say, "Goodbye." I was sitting there by myself...real scared.

What can I do to get rid of some of this scaredness? I know what Granny would do...pray.

Right then I shut my eyes and began to pray in my mind. As clear as day, my mind was covered by a picture of some words written on a little white piece of paper with light and dark blue flowers all around it. The words said, "Lo, I am with you always." For some strange reason, I felt I should close my hands real tight. When the secretary called my name to see the principal, my right hand got real warm like God was squeezing it, or something. I jes' squeezed back and whispered, "Well, here we go, jes' You and me."

I know You won't protect me all the time God, but sometimes its prob'ly like Granny says, "you jes' have to trust Him and see." Besides, what else can I do, right now? The saints would have a lot to talk about, seeing me like this.

This principal was nothing like Mr. Rowell. He was a kind looking dark skin man with a little round belly, pretty eyes and mixed gray hair in his mustache and on his head. He was prob'ly a grandfather. I could jes' see him sitting with his grandchildren propped on his knee and him smiling at them while he read them a bedtime story like Cousin Sissy used to do me when I was little. He even talked to me like I was grownup.

"When students come from the South, they generally need to be put back a grade. But since you have nothing but "A"s on your report card, I know you will be able to handle 10th grade work. If you have any problems, be sure to come and see me," Principal Jordan said.

For the first time since I came north, my fuzzy pictures began to clear. School was working its magic. Before I completed the next breath, the principal stood up and called somebody to show me to my classroom. When I got there, I was struck dumb.

Never before had I ever even seen a White teacher in with Negro children. When I looked through the door at that White man, I shivered from thoughts of the night the Klu Klux Klan came past our house in their white-sheet, truck caravan after burning a cross in Mr. Jeremy's yard. They hunted down his son and hung him. I looked around the room and saw lots of Negro kids and the teacher was still smiling, so I thought it might be alright to go in.

When Mr. Kern saw me standing in the doorway, he stopped talking, came and stood right in front of me and said, "Welcome!" with a big smile I knew was jes' for me. It was the biggest smile I had ever seen on a White or Negro man's face. He took me to the front of the room.

"Class, this is Robin. Say "Hello" and make her feel at home with us."

That made me all warm inside.

In the room, I sat in the middle of the third row from the door, exactly four seats from the front. On one side of me was a Negro girl and a White girl sat on the other. There was an empty seat behind me. But in front of me, was the most gorgeous boy who ever lived. He was White, but his skin was almost as dark as mine.

Ooooo oo, what a tan! He is darker than Jane used to look when she came home from her vacations in Florida.

Bobby was an Italian boy. He had black, black hair with eyelashes longer than any I had ever seen on any boy, even in the movie-star magazines. When he turnt around smiling and said, "Hi," my mind's pictures went blank. I couldn't say a word back to him. I know he prob'ly thought I was dumb or something. Maybe even retarded.

Each time I got near Bobby, my mind filled up with a squall of rain and my mouth was hard to move. All we ever really said to each other was "Hi" and "How are you!" Now and then in class I would have to sit with him so we could check each other's work. I was glad. Hoped that way he would see I was really smart. At my brother's birthday party, I hoped and prayed the bottle would point to me when he was spinning it, but that never happened.

Bobby's family moved to the suburbs the next summer. I never even got a chance to say, "Goodbye." For a long, long time after, I thought about him a lot and would get that warm feeling inside. It was nothing like the "Barker fire," though. Jes' warm and cozy-like.

◄▲►▼

One day when I got home from school, there was a woman in the house talking to my father and his wife. I could tell by the look on my father's wife's face that something was wrong.

Oh God, something happened to Granny! Please, please don't let her be sick...or dead!

I didn't know what to do, so I squeezed my right hand real tight and opened the door. I had to force myself to go all the way in.

"Come on in Robin. I have been waiting to talk with you," the White lady said.

"Yes ma'am."

What Miss Sally told me was that my father and his wife had got a lawyer.

Oh Lord Granny! They're trying to take me away from you!

But, since Granny had adopted me, the State said I had to go back and live with her until I was eighteen. If I even wanted to take a vacation to another State, I would have to get permission from the Courthouse. By the time Miss Sally was finished, I knew two things: One, I was an adopted child. Two, I had to go back to Granny's for at least the next two years.

How could I be adopted and not know it? Does that mean Mamma is not my real mamma? Did they get me from somewhere else and jes' not telling me? Will they ever tell me where I really came from? Where I really belong? Is Cousin Sissy my real cousin?

By Easter, I was in the kitchen teaching Granny to make Peachberry Rapture. One of my regrets was that I had forgotten to bring my records of Ferante and Tiecher playing their pianos that I loved listening to when I wanted to get quiet and dream about good stuff.

I also hated leaving the library behind, since I knew I couldn't go to the one in Shetland. For me, there is no better place in the whole wide world. It is the only place, other than in the chinaberry tree where I can jes'... "Be." The library is quiet. People don't clutter it up with a bunch of sass and gossip. But the best thing is, it's got all kinds of books.

Did you know that in books, you can do anything? Go anywhere? You can be a part of any family and even live in their house. Decorating books let me choose jes' how I want my house to look one day... right now, even. Why I can look into other folk's clothes closets, get what I want and dress up any way I want for my date. Maybe with a prince! No! Really!

Shucks, all I have to do is look at pictures, read and dream. These are things I loooove to do.

Granny and I talked and talked. She told me all about what Mamma was doing. That she had married and I had two little sisters. But by the time of my high school graduation, Mamma was divorced. I didn't get to see my new father but two times.

Thank you Mamma for bringing my sisters to hear me give my speech, since I'm the class Valedictorian.

▲ ▶ ◀ ▼

The church was packed. My speech was almost at the end of the program. I was so nervous. Knees? Shaking…hard. Real hard. I don't know why, since I knew most of the people in the church. Had known them since I was little. They had known me all my life, too.

I had practiced my speech a trillion, zillion times, but that didn't keep me from being scared. The closer it got to my place on the program, the more I shook. When it was finally my turn, I don't remember how I got to the podium. Standing there, I pretended I was Miss Ida B. Wells Barnett making a speech to get money for her Anti-lynching Campaign. That made it easy for me to open my mouth.

I said every word jes' the way I knew Miss Wells would. When I knew she would make her voice rise, mine rose. When I knew she would raise her hand, I raised mine. It was almost like I was her. The noise from people clapping brought me back.

The day after graduation when we had finished eating dinner, Mamma asked if I wanted to go back with her. You know I have wanted to live with Mamma for a long time. I forgot about that ol' college Mrs. Terrell had had me accepted to.

"Yes, yes Mamma I want to go!"

A week later, Mamma, my sisters and I boarded the Trailblazers bus and we went on our way. Finally, I was going home with Mamma where I belonged.

◀▲▼▶

Mamma lived in an apartment on the fifth floor of a twelve-story building in what they called "the projects." Our apartment had two bedrooms. One bedroom was Mamma's. All four of us girls were set up to sleep in the other room.

In our room, there was only space for the two sets of stacked beds and one chest. We had to put the other chest in the part of the closet where my baby sister's clothes hung. The oldest one of my three sisters and I slept on the top beds and the "knee baby" slept on one of the bottom beds. The other bottom bed was left free for when the baby grew some more and no longer needed to sleep in Mamma's room.

Wonder if Granny knows what 'bunk beds' are? Maybe so, since she comes up North to the church convention every year.

The rest of the apartment was a large room that was the kitchen, dining and living room altogether. When you came in from the hallway, you walked right into that room as soon as you opened the door.

A good thing about living on the fifth floor was the view. It was almost like sitting in the chinaberry tree, watching stuff. A bad thing was that sometime the elevator got stuck while you were riding up and you had to wait hours for somebody to come.

I started looking for a job right away. Mamma was on the welfare and that meant she got a check with jes' enough money in it so she and my sisters could eat and have somewhere to sleep. I was another mouth to feed. I needed to work.

Like everybody else who was not on "the grant," I had to hide when the worker came. If the worker knew I was staying with Mamma, she would have her "cut off," especially after I started working behind the counter in the drugstore and Mamma didn't report it. If the worker came unexpected, I had to hide fast.

Once on one of my off days, it happened. The worker decided to inspect.

"Who is it," Mamma said when she heard the knock.

"Miss Taylor, your caseworker, Miss Talbin!"

Hearing the worker's voice, Mamma pointed toward the room, I ran and layed on the bed where I could finish reading my story in the True Confession magazine. Felt like I know a trapped rat must feel.

Soon as I settled in, I heard the worker's footsteps coming toward our room. I jumped up off the bed and hid in the closet. The worker stuck her head in the door, but closed it back when she saw my sister taking her nap.

Tell me this: Why do people think True Confessions are nasty to read? They jes' have pictures of people hugging and kissing. Why is kissing and hugging bad? What better way can somebody let the other person know they love them? Maybe it's because of what I read they do when they keep kissing and kissing until their body catch the "Barker fire," hunh?

I know I can't ever be on Welfare when I get grown. I have got to do something special like Auntee Bertha said. Maybe I can sing and make records like I hear on the radio. I have to think about that. But first, I need to tell you this:

At work, there was this man that would come in every day for lunch. His name was Jerry and he couldn't talk. He always carried a little pad and pencil with him so when we wanted to say something to each other, we wrote it down. I was glad when he started walking me home everyday. He started teaching me how to talk with my hands. I was so happy to be learning something new. It was almost like being back in school.

I miss school. Wonder how it would be to go to college and be that chemist Miss Terrell said I should be. I bet I could do lots of research. Maybe find a cure that would make Jerry talk again. Or, a cure for something.

Better stop thinking about school! Mamma and the girls need me right now. Some day when Mamma's got a job and everybody is all grown up, I'll be able to take some classes or even go to college all day! For now, I'll jes' keep reading my True Confessions and books about chemistry.

Whether it felt good or not, I knew I had to stay with Mamma and my sisters. So I settled for work to home. Home to work.

Coming home after working late one night, I saw lots of kids my age on the playground. I jes' said, "Hi!" as I walked by. Most of them said, "Hi!" back to me. The boys whistled that didn't have a girlfriend waiting on the Monkey Bars. The boy who whistled and his girlfriend was on the bars, got a whopping upside his head in a hurry. The next night, I asked Mamma if we could all go outside.

"What?...Why?"

"It's hot up here. Could all of us go outside and cool off for a little while before we go to bed?"

"Okay. It might be nice to go out for a little while."

I couldn't believe how many people were out. The playground was filled with teenagers like me, playing their transistor radios. Blankets were spread all over everywhere with grownups sitting together eating, drinking, laughing and talking. You'd have thought there was a Mayday going on at night.

Mamma didn't want to stay long, because it was my sisters' bedtime. But I knew I had to start going to the playground when I got off work. Prayed Mamma would let me. She did.

For a time, I felt like living with Mamma was the best place in the world. Sitting on the top of the monkey bars was almost like the chinaberry tree. The only problem I had was opening my drawer in our chest of drawers to get clothes for work and finding out that my sister, Eileen, had worn my last pair of clean panties.

How in the world does Eileen keep my panties from falling down her legs? She must be a pin genius.

I didn't mind Eileen much, since we were family and all. Sisters are supposed to share.

◀▼▶▲

"I'll be glad when I turn 16 and can quit school," I heard this girl say one night. She lived in the building next to where we lived. When I heard that, I knew I had to find out why anybody would want to quit school. I definitely couldn't understand why a pretty girl like Judy wouldn't love school and want to graduate, unless she was going to run away to be a movie star like Jane. I knew she was smart. I had heard her talk. One night, I jes' walked up to her and said, "Hi." You would have thought Judy and I had known each other for years the way we talked after that.

Though almost two-years younger than I was, Judy knew things; grownup things that I had never even heard of before. I always learned a lot listening to her talk. She even smoked cigarettes and drank some kind of nasty wine called…ummmm, somebody's farms, or she would drink Richard's Rose. Judy was fun. Lots of fun. We met on the playground every night and talked until Mamma called me in. She even taught me some stuff about talking like Miss Burnice had.

"Robin, please don't say "jes'" and "turnt" when you're on the playground. It makes you sound so Country."

"But 'just,' jes' don't sound right and 'turned' is hard to say."

"But it is the right thing to say. If you keep hanging around me, you've got to say 'just' and 'turned.' Girl, I can't have people laughing at you and calling my friend "Country!"

"Oh, alright."

It was Judy who first told me about hookers and pimps, too. One night, she actually introduced me to a pimp. His name was Marvin and he had two "ho's" in his "stable." When Marvin first heard that I was "a nice girl from down South," he tried to talk to me. But Judy told him:

"Alright Marvin, you can be crazy if you want to. But she's seventeen. You know what that means. If you try anything, her mamma will put your behind under the jail."

After that, Marvin would just tease me all the time.

"Hold on to that stuff 'til you get married, Redbone. Guys out here like me, think it's always hot and ready," Marvin would say all the time. He always made me feel out of place. Most times, I hardly understood what he said. Didn't know why he called me "Redbone," for a real long time. Finally I asked him and he told me, laughing.

One night, Marvin took me and Judy with him to his stable to check on his ho's. When we got there, all I saw was these two pretty young girls who lived in the house with him. I braced myself so that I wouldn't have my mouth wide opened scared to talk when the two old ho-hags came in the room. I couldn't believe it when I found out I had already met the 'ho's. One of them had the cutest little baby boy you ever wanted to see.

How can women that pretty sell themselves to men for money? Why would they want to?

"I work the streets to take care of my baby," Marvin's 'ho told me like she was real proud. I never heard her name.

Huh! She could have a grant like Mamma until she finish a trade. There are all kinds of trades she can take up that won't take long. The counselor told me that last week. Maybe when I finish the trade I decide to take, I'll come back and show her. What kind of home will that little boy have with filthy-mouth Marvin for his daddy...father, or whatever? That sweet baby is sure to learn all of the wrong things."

Can you tell me why ho's are so happy to turn their money over to their pimps? They even brag about how sharp their pimp is dressed and the kind of car their pimp drives. I guess I could understand ho'ing if the women were doing something they love to do. But they don't love it. Want to know how I know? Every time I see a 'ho, she always look tired and sad. When you're doing what you love, you don't look like that.

Marvin's 'ho with the baby bragged and bragged. The more she bragged, the sadder she looked in her eyes. I knew that that was definitely no kind of life for me. Even though she lived in a house with a "husband" and baby like I want to, I could tell that her house was no place she could go for rest when every place else in the world got crazy. There wasn't even a chinaberry tree in the yard.

Where?   Where? Oh, where?

PART III

MRS. G

◀ ▼ ▶ ▲

Judy introduced me to my husband. We were sitting on the playground swings when she asked.

"Want to tag along with me tonight?

I answered, "Where you going?"

"To the Magic Beanery. Wanna come?"

"Judy. Girl are you going somewhere else to eat? I just finished eating. I'm full," contentedly rubbing my belly.

"The Magic Beanery ain't no restaurant, silly, it's a coffeehouse!" Then sounding just like she lived over in England, Judy said, "I need a spot of tea!" with her little finger stuck up in the air.

I didn't really know what a coffeehouse was. But after Judy told me it was a place where people sat and talked while they drank coffee and tea, I wanted to go.

I really wanted to go, though, when she told me there would probably be somebody playing the guitar, singing and reciting poetry. Hadn't really heard any poems since Cousin Sissy used to say them to me back in Shetland. I hadn't been where I could hear people sing since Cousin Russell had me singing in the Pego clubs with his band.

It sure sounds like fun. Wonder if they will let me sing a song or two?

Singing in the nightclubs in Pego was nothing like how Judy described the coffeehouse. The coffeehouse seemed all cozy and warm, not filled with thick smoke and people drinking, yelling and clowning.

When we got to the coffeehouse, sure enough it was just like what I imagined, except we had to sit down on pillows around this table real low to the floor. Looking around, I saw all the smiling, friendly faces in hushed conversation.

"Wow Judy, this is great," I whispered so nobody would be disturbed. But boy was I disturbed when I looked up and saw walking toward us the finest six-foot, dark brown frame I had ever seen. He got closer and closer and the shimmer in his light, brown eyes got brighter and brighter. When he smiled…"Wow, magic!"

The sparkle from his teeth lights up his face like Mamma's! He walks kind of like Keith.

"Hi Judy, what's happening?"

"Nothing shaking, man. Just hanging out with my bud, Roe."

It was Judy's friend, Jeff.

"Oh that's right, you two don't know each other. Robin, Jeff. Jeff, well…the other way around."

I turned to look up and say, "Nice to meet you," but something happened when my eyes met Jeff's. They got stuck. The next thing I knew…"Hey, I want some Black Bean Cocoanut Dream, if you two don't mind," I heard Judy yelling.

"Coming right up," Jeff answered, kind of awkward like. He broke his gaze and left without ever asking for my order. I wondered what he would bring me. Was too mushy inside to insist on ordering.

"Hey Roe, so you think Jeff is cute, huh?"

I just grunted my agreement. Couldn't talk, yet.

When Jeff brought our tea to the table, he stood and talked to Judy for a while without ever looking at me. I just glanced at him now and then out of the corner of my eye and smiled in the right places to what they said. Kept my mouth filled with tea, so they would see I couldn't talk. Knew I would sound dumb if I did.

Though I didn't hear much of what else they talked about, I heard when Jeff asked if Judy and I would come watch him play baseball that Saturday. "Yes" popped through my lips like answers used to do in Shetland Elementary. When I heard it, I quickly put my hand over my mouth, but too late.

"Well alright then, I guess we're coming," Judy said with a smile and wink.

Floor, why don't you ever open up and swallow me? Every time I do, or say something dumb and stupid, you just make me sit in place looking dumb and stupid.

Judy and I were having so much fun at the baseball game that I forgot to watch for signs that Jeff thought I was dumb. Judy yelled or moaned for every play the teams made. After a while, I got in the spirit and yelled, too. We really yelled when Jeff's team won. Then we all piled into one of the team-member's car and headed for the playground to celebrate. Jeff stayed near me the whole time. When it was time for me to go inside, he asked if I would come to the coffeehouse the next night.

I went to the coffeehouse almost every night Jeff worked, after that. The first few times, Judy was with me. Then, I got up the nerve to go by myself.

Nights Jeff didn't work, he came to the playground. When Mamma beckoned me inside, he walked me to the lobby. We'd hug our friendly hug when we heard the elevator coming. Before long, Jeff stayed with me all the way to my door and Mamma made it clear that he could always come in.

The first time Jeff kissed me goodnight, it was nice. Kind of soft, sweet and warm. But a "Barker fire?" Nooooooo!

One night, Jeff gave me a strange hug in the elevator. I knew something was about to happen. He was too stiff.

"What's wrong?"

"Nothing much."

"Nothing much? What does that mean? Come on Jeff. Whatever it is, you can surely tell me."

"Rovie, I won't see you for a while. Going down South for my family's reunion."

I was relieved it was just that, but couldn't imagine what I would do with myself while Jeff was gone. Judy would be too busy with her new boyfriend, Billy, to walk me in when Mamma beckoned. She might not even be on the playground.

What if somebody messes with me on the elevator or pop out of the stairwell door and grab me like they did that girl in building 409?

For a couple of days after Jeff left, I felt like I know children in orphanages must feel: deserted, dejected and desolate without their mamma or a granny. Probably had no right to feel that way, since I knew Jeff would be back soon. But I did. When I got home from work, I still went outside. A few nights later, Rocco Gonzales, a Mexican boy Judy worked with brought a new boy to the playground.

Sam had come from Africa with his father, the king. They had come for the naming ceremony of his cousin, the baby of the king's sister. Rocco thought Sam would enjoy meeting everybody.

Finally, I get to meet somebody who actually lives in Africa! Yea! He's not just somebody, but a real African prince. Can you believe it?

I know <u>you</u> know how I felt. I have been talking to you about Africa for a long time now.

From the second Sam and I met, we had something special. We talked easy and there was something about his voice that made my insides giggle. He was taller than Jeff, long and lanky, and his smooth, smooth skin was so blue-black it glowed, even at night. His teeth? A perfect white. That was the first time I had met anybody who walked like walking was real, real good to them, since Keith Barker. Every time Sam took a step, I imagined him running with the herd of gazelles on the April cover of the nature magazine.

Mamma must've forgotten me tonight, I thought one night. But before my joy about getting to spend extra time talking with Sam could take hold, I saw her in the window.

"Yo Mommee waint'cha ta come eenside?"

"Yes. It was nice talking with you, but I have to go. Come back again before you leave, if you can. I would love to talk to you some more about your home."

"I will wa'k ya een, eef ya don' mind."

I thought Sam would just go to the elevator, but when it opened, he got on with me. As soon as the door closed, he grabbed and kissed me, one of those French ones. At first I stiffened and tried to push away screaming, "What are you doing?"

He didn't try to kiss me, anymore that time. Just stood there holding me real close. Like magic, even without kissing, I started to get real hot from "Barker fire" rushing all over my body. It went over me faster than how I read fire spreads when men who live in African villages set fire to dead grass fields to flush out their catch for meals.

In the distance, I heard a noise and somehow realized that the elevator had stopped and the door was opened. I pushed Sam away and waited for Miss Hazel to walk on.

We had missed my floor two floors below. I pushed the fifth-floor button and waited stiffly near the door. Sam said something, but I don't know what. Soon as the door opened, I whispered "Bye" real quick and ran toward my door that Mamma was holding wide opened on her way out to get me. I breezed right pass her to my room and by the time she closed the door, had jumped into bed, clothes and all. It was a while before I caught my breath and settled my nerves.

Every night after that, Sam came to the playground and went in with me when it was time. I looked forward to it, by the third time. We went into the lobby earlier and earlier, sometimes not even waiting for Mamma to appear at the window. Those times, I wanted Judy to let me know when Mamma beckoned, but she wouldn't.

"Girl, are you crazy? My bud Jeff will be back next week and what exactly will I tell him?"

But Sam and I found a way without her help.

If somebody else was waiting for the elevator, instead of getting on Sam and I waited for the next one. While we were on the elevator, if someone got on, we'd get off and walk to the stairwell, hoping we'd not be interrupted there. If someone did come up or down the stairs, we went and stood in front of the elevator, again.

One night, we got off the elevator on the sixth floor and walked around to the stairwell on the side where I could best hear if Mamma opened the door to go out looking for me, after she didn't see me on the playground. As soon as the stairwell door closed, Sam hoisted my t-shirt and bra with one swoop and began kissing my tits. Amazingly, it didn't scare me and when he nibbled my nipple, a strange chill covered my body and a moan popped out of my mouth. I could hear somebody knocking on a door, but it seemed far, far away in a dream world. Moans and pants were Sam and my only reality. Only what I heard, brought me back.

"Good evening Mrs. Talbin. Is Rovie, I mean Robin home? She wasn't on the playground, so I thought she might be up here."

"Nope, Robin didn't come in, yet, Jeff. Maybe she went to Judy's. Did you check there?

"Yes Ma'am."

"How's your family? How was your reunion? You'll have to tell me about it sometimes. You want to come in and wait? You can tell me all about it right now."

"Yes Ma'am, if you don't mind."

Hearing Jeff's voice, I froze. Only after I heard the door close did I even exhale.

"I have to go," I whispered loudly.

"Whyyyyy," Sam asked as he grabbed me in a hold that hardly allowed me breath. For every "I have to go," Sam said, "No," each time with more and more force. The final "noooooo" came through clenched teeth.

Scared…I did what had to be done: I put my foot on the wall, quickly pushed real hard, while jerking my arms outward. The force knocked Sam to the floor. I ran down the stairs like greased lightening. With the stairwell door opened, I looked back just in time to see Sam scrambling to get up.

"Thank goodness," I whispered. The apartment door was unlocked. Quickly, I opened and shut it as I ran toward the bathroom, throwing a "Hi Jeff, you're back" over my shoulder. Needed some time to get myself together. I knew Mamma and Jeff would think I had to "use it" real bad, since I was coming from outside.

After that night, I never saw Sam again. Rocco said he had gone back home. Didn't matter, because Jeff and I were spending all our free time together, anyway.

▼ ▲ ◀ ▶

One Saturday after Jeff finished his baseball game, he suggested we walk to the fountain in the park. While standing there snuggled in each other's arms watching the fountain turn from red to blue, Jeff asked.

"Rovie, will you marry me?"

I was so thrilled I said the only thing I could.

"Yes! Yes!"

There was just one problem with getting married soon, the way Jeff wanted: In July I was taking my sisters to visit Granny for the month. I wouldn't postpone that trip even for Jeff. Granny was ailing and she needed me. Besides, it was the time when everybody would expect me to "Come on back home for Family Reunion" like the letter had said.

Every time we talked, Jeff hounded me to set the date. He insisted we get married before I left for Shetland. Though hearing his pleas made me feel real good, each time he asked, I told him we had to wait.

"If you don't want to marry me before you leave, you must not love me" was added to Jeff's plea.

I gave in.

Jeff and I married two days before my sisters and I left. Since neither of us had saved any money, we were married in the Pastor's study of a little storefront, by a minister Jeff had known since he was a little boy. Jeff looked real handsome in his new navy pants, light blue shirt and the finest red and blue tie I had ever seen. I knew he had bought all that to match my royal blue organza dress with the tips of the sash that tied in the front, dipped in red.

For Jeff and me, there was nobody else in the room from the time the preacher spoke the first word. I heard little of what was said. I am sure Jeff didn't hear much either as we got lost in each other's souls. "You may kiss your bride," made me see Jeff's mom, Kim, his brother Jamar, Mamma and her boyfriend, Cal, standing there with beaming smiles. After everything was over, we all went back to Mamma's house.

"Surprise, surprise" everybody yelled the moment we opened the door. It was certainly a surprise. We thought we were sneaking. I hadn't told anybody outside of family, but Judy. Jeff said he only told his family. But apparently, that was enough to spread the word.

That night, we partied real hard. Food had been ordered from the Chinese place around the corner and Judy had had one of her friends help her cook lots of stuff. Wine, beer and booze cooled in the kitchen sink. There was a sheet cake decorated with a bride and groom and we even got presents.

Mamma gave us her bedroom for the night. When she said, "Ya'll keep the sheets," everybody's laughter bellowed.

Judy gave us her present last. She handed it to Jeff with a big Cheshire-cat grin like she knew something we didn't.

"Don't unwrap this until you are in the room by yourselves," she whispered. That made me think it might be one of those sexy toys she had showed me. But when we broke the wrapper open, it was just two books, "The Tropic of Cancer" and "The Secret Garden."

"Rovie, why would Judy think we would want to read about cancer when we just got married?"

"I don't know. But I do know there certainly ain't no place for us to plant a garden in these Projects,"

Jeff tossed the books on the dresser, climbed across me to the other side of the bed, took me in his arms and held me close. We fell asleep like that, all snuggled up tight. When I woke up, there was Jeff looking deep into my eyes.

"Good morning Mrs. Jeffrey Gibson."

"Good morning Mr. Jeffrey Gibson," I said in my sexiest imitation of the bedroom voice I had heard that actress, Talullah Bankhead, use. We kissed and the "Barker fire" spread over my body. Jeff felt it too and I was glad. It was the happiest I had been since when I won first prize in the State for typing 101 words a minute with two errors and taking dictation at 105. That made Granny real happy. It made me happy, too.

I will make Jeff just as happy in our home as my winning made Granny, I repeated in my mind until it was a part of my soul.

▼ ▶ ▲ ◀

All the way to Shetland, I dreamed of ways to make Jeff happy. I dreamed just how our family and home would be.

We will have two boys and two girls. I will be a real good mother and Jeff will be a father who is always hugging and doing different things to keep me and our children grinning from ear to ear. I will make our home real pretty, too.

I could almost smell the fresh, bleach scent of the white curtains with tiny purple flowers. Could see their ruffles slowly waving in the gentle breeze blowing through the kitchen window. The remembered taste of Peachberry Rapture cooling on the table, tickled my taste buds. Thought about the children playing with their toys near the door, just waiting for their daddy to walk through. Jeff would come in smiling, pick them up, giving each a big hug teaming with fatherly passion. He saves his manly passion for after they are in bed and he pulls me into his arms and fill me up with his luscious, long, loving kisses.

We will be a loving, happy family. Granny will be proud to come visit our home. She will come and spend her month in....

"Hey! Hey! Hey! A-i-n'-c-h-y'a-l-l 'sp-o-s-e ta g-i d-o-f-f a-' t-h-a Sh-e-'-l-a-n-d s-t-o-p?"

The bus driver's voice shocked me out of my dreaming. I jumped up and was gathering our bags when I looked out the window and saw Granny and Uncle James craining their necks trying to see us.

Granny hugged my sisters three times soon as we stepped off the bus. Me, she hugged a fourth. When we were in Uncle James' car and I told her I was married and showed her Jeff's picture, she smiled a happy smile. But her friend, one of the saints I call Aunt Lou, wasn't happy when I told her. Know what she said to me?

"Roe-Roe, I don' thank you really love yo' husband. Efen you did, you wouldna come way off down here and lef' him way up yondah. You sho' wouldn' be stayin' 'way from him so long an' ya'll jes' got married."

That was the first time I ever thought whether what I felt for Jeff was "real love." I knew I wanted to be with him and that when I was with him it felt like I belonged. When we kissed, I even felt the "Barker fire."

What is "real love" suppose to feel like anyway? However it feels, do Jeff and I have to have it to be happy together?

I worried about "real love" so much over the next few weeks, I made myself sick. My stomach started flopping around and I felt dizzy. Uncle James and Granny took me to a place I had always dreaded...the Shetland hospital.

"Oh Lord, don't let them White doctors kill me, please!" was my whispered prayer from the time we left the house, until I heard the doctor coming into the room. My right hand was squeezed real tight. From there, came shock.

This short, but handsome Black man strolled into the room with a stethoscope wrapped around his neck. I checked his name badge twice to make sure I saw E. Nelson, MD. After the examination, Dr. Nelson and I spent a little time just talking.

"How did you get to Shetland? No, how did you get to be a doctor at Shetland General?"

Dr. Nelson understood my disbelief. His presence had been questioned, lots.

"A doctor my grandmother helped to raise, told me to apply and here I am," he said in a soothing voice. But my fears were not calmed.

Doctor Nelson asked me about my life up North and about Jeff. When he said he didn't find anything wrong with me, all of my senses went on alert. I started thinking a little crazy.

Wait a minute here. Now, I am am Black. Have the White doctors brainwashed Dr. Nelson like the Germans did in the War? Maybe they programmed him to send me home, even if I am really sick. Growing up, I heard the old folks talk about how Negroes would always be sent home to tend themselves or die so the two hospital beds assigned them were free in case they were needed for somebody White.

I relaxed a little though, after the doctor said, "Mrs. Gibson, let me suggest you never go anyplace for a long period of time without your husband." Hesitantly, I told him I wouldn't. When the long busride from Shetland ended, the bus door opened and I saw Jeff waiting with his arms opened wide, as soon as I was in them, I knew I would keep my word.

Jeff and I moved in with his mother until we could save enough money for our own place. We went back to the Projects often, so I kept my friendship with Judy. Before long, Judy got married and we were both sporting big bellies.

"Judy, those books are responsible for my belly. What's your excuse?"

"Girl, you and Jeff were so 'green' that I had to do something. I figured one book would heat you up and the other would show you two how to cool off the right way."

Of all the wedding gifts, Judy's had turned out to be the best. Jeff and I read those books over and over and tried most of the stuff in them. Eventhough we were young and flexible, some of those positions were just impossible.

Between you and me, I know somebody just thought up some stuff, wrote it down and drew pictures. I tell you this though: Anytime Jeff and I followed those books, we poured moans into each other's ears.

I could hear Granny saying, "Wait 'til you get married. Those feelings are worth waiting for, Roe-Roe!"

She was right. *D-e-f-i-n-i-t-e-l-y!*

It still boggles my mind to think that those books were banned and somebody actually had to smuggle them into the Country. They should be handed out with every marriage license.

▶▲◀▼

After paining from 2:00 o'clock in the afternoon, at 4:10 the next morning our daughter, Elizabeth, was born. Having had real bad monthly cramps, I thought I knew pain. But, nooooo! Let me tell you: You don't know pain until you have had your bones separating for hours while your insides toss and turn to make a passage big enough for a nine pound baby!

I knew I would surely die. But when I looked into Ellie's face and felt her little fingers and tiny toes, I knew it had all been worth it. When Jeff and I hugged with Ellie between us, we looked deeply into each other's eyes and at almost the same time said, "perfect."

Want to hear something funny? Listen to this:

The night of my labor, Jeff was so tired that he actually slept while I timed my pains. When the pains were five minutes apart, I woke him up singing, "It's hospital tiiiime!"

"What? Can't it wait? Can't it wait 'til in the morning?"

Jeff's next breath was the loudest snore, ever. I shook him and repeated my statement again, more sing-songy than before. This time, Jeff jumped up.

"It's what, Rove? Come on! Get up! We've got to hurry!"

Then he rushed into the nursery, grabbed my packed bag (and for some reason my blue robe) and bolted out of the door before I could stand up straight. Jeff told me later that just as he was locking the door, he noticed I wasn't with him. All I really know is that I looked up and Jeff was standing in the wide-opened door holding my bag with my robe draped across his arm, looking silly. He just said, "Rovie, I'm sorry," then came back in, put his arms around me and tenderly helped me to the car.

I must have had a million, zillion contractions on the way to the hospital. As the nurse was wheeling me away, there stood Jeff still holding the bag with my robe draped over his arm and the silliest look on his face. He had a look that yelled, "I don't know if I should go forward or backwards, be happy or sad, laugh or cry?" Jeff was standing there as if suspended by marionette wires. His mouth? Wide opened. The nurse thought I was suffering pain hysteria when I started laughing out loud. All it was was that my mind flashed back to when I saw Jeff standing in the door of our home and joined it with the way he was looking at that moment. I couldn't help but laugh. The louder I laughed, the faster the nurse wheeled. But the next round of contractions shut me up, but good.

Our second child, a son, was born a little over two years later. By the time Christian was born, Jeff and I were growing in different directions. I liked casserole-so did Ellie-Jeff liked hot dogs fried crisp and black. I wanted to read, Jeff wanted me to sit and watch TV with him. Said he felt lonely when he watched alone.

How much TV can one person stand to watch?

Soon, Jeff started going out for "nights with the boys." Often.

"Jeff, can I go with you next time? I get tired of staying home all the time. Now and then, I'd like to be with grownups who are laughin and having fun."

"What? You can't go with me! The boys would feel uncomfortable having my wife along!"

What about how uncomfortable I feel when you're not home, I thought. *Do you ever think about that?* But I never let a peep come through my lips.

Every time the phone rang when Jeff was out, I'd shudder thinking something had happened to him. I had heard what S.T.R.A.P. did when they caught young Black men out at night. I knew how policemen could be. Sheriff Black Bart showed me that a long time ago in Shetland. S.T.R.A.P. was one special police unit not known for its protecting and helping ways.

As soon as my eyes opened one morning, I knew something was wrong. Jeff was not home. For three days, I didn't see or hear from him. I called his friends, the police and hospitals. When he didn't turn up, I started thinking how it would be caring for my children alone. The thought scared me so badly that I could only move if Ellie and Chris needed me to. I didn't wash myself or get dressed for the first two days, just prayed a lot and tended my children.

On the third day, I awakened from the dream of a strong me who could do what I knew I had to. Saw myself in the morning, getting my children to the sitter, working all day and having plenty of energy left for hugging and playing in the evening. All day I replayed that dream in my mind. Replayed it so much that at some point, I wasn't sure it was a dream.

"Da Da! Da Da!" Chris yelled. Excited, he jumped up and down on the couch. Jeff was coming up the walkway. Seeing me in the window, he smiled a smile that at one time would have warmed my heart. This time, it froze my feelings so solid that if they had fallen to the floor right then, one misstep would have sent me sliding back as far as Shetland with slithers still left unthawed.

Of course I asked Jeff where he had been. You want to know what he said? Listen to this one: "I was kidnapped and robbed." When I asked, "By whom?" No answer.

"Where did you get money for the fresh haircut and new shirt?"

"Oh, they gave me my money back this morning. Rovie. What did you expect me to do? I'm only human!"

One thing I can say, "There is no half-truth for Jeff." But I didn't know how to respond to a lie that big. So, I just kept as quiet as I could, watched and waited. It was near Christmas and I didn't want to make any rash moves that would cast a shadow over Ellie and Chris's good time. That was the first Christmas Ellie was old enough to really enjoy. I wanted it to be special.

Every time Jeff tried to justify his disappearance, I simply said, "Oooooh, I see" in a tone filled with more and more anger and frustration. After a while, I am sure I sounded much like the first turn of a rusty, frozen wagon wheel when I said it. In my head though, I started making plans for me and my children's future…without Jeff.

The first thing I knew I had to do was return to school. Not only so I could get a job that would support two children, but also to clear my head. I knew I could count on school for the clarity I needed…real bad.

◀ ▼ ▶ ▲

A little before Ellie's third birthday, I started classes. Not having Jeff around to help anymore, I thought it best to take an apartment in the Projects. That way, I would be near Mamma and my sisters if I needed help. I don't know how I would have made it without them in the first few months. My sisters helped me with the children and I helped them with their homework. If I didn't have class, I would even go to their parent-teacher conferences and other activities. After my second semester of classes, though, Jeff got layed off and I had to stop school.

What can I do now? Should I take a job and forget about school? Can't put my children on welfare. I won't have them feeling like "poor Projects kids." Besides, Granny warned me and Mamma showed me about that.

But wait. Is it that children feel worthless when they are on welfare? Or, is it that parents pass their feelings of hopelessness on to their children? Maybe Welfare is not so bad if I use it temporarily, just to finish school. That way, I can become a working, productive taxpayer. Can even make my children feel more secure by owning my own home. I need to work this out.

I took a job.

My first job was assisting an accountant. My excitement at having a "good" job" made me grin a lot, especially every time I thought about how I had escaped working in the mill and the Company Store down in Shetland.

"See Shetland people, there is some other kind of work to do!"

Little did I know that my "good job" would take over my life. I had to balance books and send the balance sheets to each of the companies on my account list every single week. After a while, my load increased and balancing took longer and longer. There were weeks when I worked 14-hour days and on weekends, which meant I saw less and less of Ellie and Chris. When I did, either I was so tired I couldn't give them the attention they wanted or I was totally distracted, still trying to figure out what I missed that made the numbers not balance.

Ouch! How in the world? I know I need to make a move now.

I was on my second pair of glasses. The doctor had prescribed heavy-duty drugs in an effort to control my headaches. The pills made me smack into a pole I had been walking around all the time.

Walking into that pole was a good thing. It woke me up. I handed in my resignation and cleaned out my desk. Didn't even worry about what I would do next. The medication and pressure of constantly balancing the books made my pictures too fuzzy to make any life decisions, anyway. Instead, I focused on the opportunity I had to get welfare while I took the classes needed to finish my degree. Also, I would get to spend more time with Ellie and Chris.

▲ ◀ ▼ ▶

I enjoyed being a full-time mom again. My sister, Eileen, moved in with us so I could take classes at night. Wanted to be home for Ellie and Chris during the daytime.

The children and I hugged, played, and laughed.

Wait, wait! Let me breathe! Don't tickle Mommie anymore!

Stop Mommie, stop! Ellie's stomach hurt!

Besides playing, I had time to help Ellie recognize letters and numbers. Would put them into words and problems when she asked, "Mommie, let's play with numbers and letters, pleeeese?" No matter what I was doing, when Ellie asked, I stopped. By her fourth birthday, she could dial telephone numbers and by the first day of Kindergarten, could read.

During my first parent-teacher conference, the teacher complained that Ellie spent most of her day in the play area. I arranged a conference and observation (as parents were encouraged to do), hoping to see if there was something I should do at home to resolve whatever the problem was. What I saw that afternoon was discouraging.

The teacher had the children watch a movie. Now, there are times I don't understand Peter Max. When the teacher questioned the children about the movie (which I know was for my benefit), they didn't understand Peter Max either.

My next school observation was unscheduled and in the morning. I wanted to know what a full day was like for Ellie.

I know why Ellie spends her time in the play area, now.

The teacher gave the children a duplicated sheet to trace a letter and a sheet with a big picture to color. Ellie finished those in a snap.

"Mrs. Gibson, today the children are learning the sounds letters make. That is a precursor to reading," the teacher told me.

I was real happy that I knew the meaning of the word "precursor." Otherwise, I probably would have gone home thinking my Ellie was doing something extra special.

"But Ellie is already reading."

Without a word the teacher snatched a book from her desk.

"If you can read, here, read this," she said, shoving the book into Ellie's hands with such force it begged attention.

Ellie looked longingly at me for a moment, then started sounding out the words the way we had played. You would have thought Ellie and I were threatening the teacher's life from the way she reacted. I was shocked when instead of encouraging Ellie, the teacher started scolding me for helping her.

"For Ellie's sake, Mrs. Gibson, let me do the teaching! Parents teach children one way, then they come to school and I teach them a different way. It confuses them."

As soon as the teacher finished, from somewhere I heard this strange high-pitched voice say a stupid sounding, "Hunh?"

I froze. Tightly clamped my lips together so my thoughts wouldn't pop out. Pictures were flashing so fast and furiously across my mind that I almost lost control, but I remembered Ellie was standing there.

Wonder where I ever got the notion that teachers and parents were suppose to work together for the good of the child? Silly me!

I know it was rage: There I was. Standing in front of this teacher with the words, "Save the children, knock this silly bitch out" floating through my mind on ticker tape. I knew I had to get out of there right then or I would say something I'd regret. So I turned and without another word to the teacher, kissed Ellie with an "I'll see you later, Sweety" and left.

On my way home, I was steadily talking to myself and <u>you</u> in my mind. May have talked aloud. If I did, I know the people I passed just thought I was a mental patient walking the streets until someone found and returned me to the hospital.

I didn't care. The questions just kept on coming. I couldn't stop them.

What's the problem here? Is it wrong for me to help Ellie do her best? Is it the teacher? This time I know I can't blame the teacher's behavior on "white teacher-black child," like with my sister's teachers. I have to deal with behavior, not color. What do I do?

I know what it is! The teacher probably didn't expect a 'Projects' child to be able to read when she started school. Didn't think a struggling single parent would take time to help. Probably didn't think I had any smarts, either.

As soon as I opened my door, I ran and took out my cards to play solitaire. Had learned in childhood that solitaire would slow my thoughts enough to give me a chance to change them. It worked. After about an hour, my thinking cleared.

What should I do? I have to do something!

I thought about changing my major from Dentistry to Education over the next few days. Felt that if I became a teacher, I could at least save some of the children.

I would make learning fun and teach the child at her ability level, not the grade or age. Certainly can't go around knocking teachers out. Besides, how would I know the good ones from the bad? In the meantime, Ellie's is just one teacher I need to stay away from.

The next time Jeff came to visit the children, I shared what had happened during my observations. Suggested that he be the observing parent as long as

Ellie was in kindergarten. He agreed to do it, then immediately began belittling my reactions.

"Rovie, the teacher can't be that bad. What was wrong with you when you went to the school that day? You must've been in one of your moods. You know how you can get sometime...moving West."

Jeff's verbal attacks were becoming more and more frequent. Much of his talk was strange, too. Something was wrong, I just knew it.

After Jeff's first observation, he reported how nice the teacher had been.

"Rove, what were you talking about? I didn't see anything wrong with Ellie's teacher. See, she even sent Ellie a book to read."

I looked at the book and saw it was a fifth-grade text. Fury took over, again. I could just see Ellie's teacher snowing Jeff under with her "Mr. Gibson" this and "Mr. Gibson" that.

Uuummmmmmmph! I know what she did! Just picked up any ol' book and handed it to Jeff. She didn't even take the time to see and probably didn't even care at what level Ellie might be reading! I know I did the right thing, asking Jeff to be school parent.

When Jeff came from an unscheduled observation though, his opinion had obviously changed. He walked in with this strange look on his face and said, "Rove, I see what you mean. Ellie needs to be out of that room." I only wondered what happened. Didn't ask and Jeff never told me. By that time, the school year was ending, so it really didn't matter. I knew I would not have to deal with that teacher again. Hoped the next one would be more nurturing.

Jeff wanted to make arrangements for Ellie to attend private school. Though I had always been vehemently opposed to even the mere notion of private school, I agreed.

Wasn't long before my world began to crumble again. I got the call that Granny was dying. Everything stopped, except the whirling in my head. I packed up my children and was on my way to Shetland.

Through the next few months, my movements and words felt and sounded as if they were being projected from the moon. I remembered little of the funeral or coming back home. Ellie and Chris were the only bright spots in my otherwise gloomy days as I maneuvered through our daily routines.

▼▲◄►

Jeff wasn't the only one slandering me. Judy and Mamma, the two people I counted on most, were terse and ridiculing, too. I don't know exactly when it started. At first notice, I just thought, *Naaw, this can't be happening. I must be seeing this wrong. Of all people, these two know the struggles I have had trying to be a good mom and keep up with my studies. They are my best friend and my mamma for goodness sakes!*

The longer I stayed in school, the more blatant Mamma and Judy's criticisms got. I would leave their presence wobbling from the weightiness that pressed my chest in the very spot where my heart used to beat warmly around them. If I said something was green, they said it was blue. If I said up, they said down. Don't let me say it should be this way, they would...well, you know what they would say. One day, Judy came right out and asked.

"Girl, when are you going to get a job and stop wasting your time in that ol' school? It's been years! Don't you see your kids need clothes?"

You know what? My children did need clothes and so did I. While I had been busy trying to keep up with school and make a good home, styles had changed. I had been spending any extra money on books. Ellie and Chris had so many books that I had to take more milk crates from behind the store across the street. Let us not mention all the books I had on my shelf and in my crates. I had a crate library not only in both our bedrooms, but one in the living room that took up almost half the wall.

When I took my children to the playground, I saw that though clean, their clothes looked like "poor Projects kids" compared to the spiffiness of the other children's clothes.

How can a 'good' mother allow her children to look like this? I need to do something.

So when Judy told me they were hiring at the supermarket where she worked, I filled out the application she brought me and went for the interview.

I hear your scolding. It won't stop me from finishing school. I can work during the day and take classes a couple of nights a week. It will take me longer to finish, but my children will not have to feel less than other children. I can't let them be teased or laughed at for the way they dress. They need to know they are as good as anybody.

Walking into Mr. White's office to interview was one of the hardest things I had done in a very long time. I tightly clutched the folder containing my application and resume with my left hand and squeezed real tight, my right. When Mr. White yelled my name, I whispered softly, "Here we go again, You and me" before I got up from the chair.

Mr. White took a look at my application, scowled at my resume and told me to wait outside. He kept me waiting for what felt like hours. I didn't mind. I had brought some reading and homework.

Just before it was time for me to pick Ellie up from school, I heard my name called again. I was filled with both excitement and dread thinking I had gotten the job. Before I got through the door, Mr. White looked at me sternly and said, "Sit down" in a way that dread outweighed excitement.

"I see you are in school."

"Yes Sir."

"Well, I want you to listen closely to what I am about to say. I am a little older than you, certainly been Black longer than you and have been in the supermarket business a long, long time. Let me give you some advice: Take yourself back to school and don't stop until I am sitting in your chair with my mouth opened saying, 'ugh.' Do you hear what I am saying?"

"Yes Sir."

Then with the same scowl on his face as when he had looked at my resume, Mr. White said, "Now bye! And don't ever let me see you in this office again! You hear me? Go get on the welfare if you have to, but don't quit school!"

I couldn't get out of there fast enough. In fact, when Judy interrupted my gait to ask if I had gotten the job, without slowing I yelled, "I'll tell you about it later!"

Mr. White knew I would not work in a supermarket for long. What he didn't know was that I am already on the welfare. Just needed to make a little extra money.

Standing at the bus stop I whispered over and over and over again, "Thank You, thank You, thank You!" I started thinking about Granny who had gone on to heaven just after Ellie's fifth birthday. Could feel her standing beside me saying, "I told you God would go before you to straighten out the rough places. All you have to do is trust Him." For the first time since dealing with the saints in Shetland, I felt she might be right.

Granny, you don't know how much I miss you. Don't know how much I need you right now. That's why it took me months to stop crying and feel I could go on. Hearing you in my mind is what helped. Seeing you in my dreams has been the only thing that has made me feel strong, again. Now I need you to tell me, should I be a dentist or a teacher?

You know the land you bought for the young people's playground? Don't worry, I will build it. But you've got to tell me what to do now!

Before the bus came, my mind filled with the notion that teaching was it. Mr. White would have to take his "ugh" elsewhere.

◀ ▶ ▼ ▲

"The best way to assure children's academic success is to in early grades, provide them well-trained teachers who enjoy what they do. Teachers are needed who can individuate learning strategies to the degree possible and are guided by each child's learning style. The best teachers are those who recognize age and grade as skill indicators only," the article read.

Wow! Somebody finally agrees with me. I have to read about this author to see if what brought her to this conclusion was anything like my experiences.

I hope when I start teaching, I will quickly learn each child in my classroom and use what I learn in a way that the child progresses and wants to continue learning. Noooo. Maybe, it would be better if I taught college. That way, I could guide would-be teachers toward new and different methods that are more likely to generate greater academic growth for many more children than I could teach on my own.

When I shared my new plan with Judy and Mamma, they looked at each other in a way that spoke louder than they could ever have, using their mouths.

"She really has flipped her lid this time," their looks said. "She is trying to change teachers. Did she forget where she is from? What school teacher is going to listen to some Black girl from the projects?"

I couldn't understand Judy. It was not like she couldn't have shared school with me. I begged her to come. Every time I asked, she said, "Naw girl, I have these children to raise. I need to try to get me a job."

One night at a party, I had heard Mamma's reply when a lady asked her how many children she had. "Three," she answered.

"I thought you had an older child."

"Oh yea," Mamma said, probably because I decided to walk into the room at that very moment.

"Hi there! I thought Cal told me you are one of the children, too."

"I am. I'm Robin. How are you?"

She was Mamma's boyfriend, Cal's, sister and he had told her I had been in school for years. That I would probably finish, since no matter what happened in my life that caused me to quit, I always went back.

"It's so nice that you are trying to make something out of yourself, 'specially since you have to raise the children by yourself."

"Thank you for the compliment."

Then I went into the party, got me a drink and danced until Mamma's open denial (forgetfulness?) no longer hurt.

The next day even with my big, fat hangover, I knew that if I chose to "make something out of myself," I would have to do it without Mamma and Judy's support.

Feeling alone is the worst, ever. I felt as if I had been dropped into an abyss and was just dangling. Not falling, just dangling. The feeling lasted for days. My mind was not only filled with fuzzy pictures, but ones pitch black around the edges. There were a few bright places in them, but no real light. The one person in the world I knew would understand, was Cousin Sissy. I hadn't talked to her in years. Didn't even know where she was. I called Aunt Mable in Shetland.

"Chil' you know Sissy lef' heah, long befo' you did. She ain't been back heah since."

"Can you ask Aunt Lou how to reach her? I know Cousin Sissy use to talk to her sometime."

"You didn' heah? Lou died months ago."

"Oh God, nooo!"

Thought about Jane. Knew where she was, but knew better than to try and contact her. Replayed in my mind that disturbing night I saw coverage of the Pennysville murder trial on TV:

The Grand Dragon and his entourage were walking up the courthouse steps. When they got to the top and turned (I guess for the cameras), next to him stood his dutiful wife, Jane. She was twice the size I remembered. I barely saw the girl I knew. Her face seemed to crack and nearly shatter when she tried to smile. Her metallic voice rattled my nerves when she answered the reporter's question with, "I guarantee my husband will be acquitted." My stomach did violent flip-flops.

Standing on the other side of the Grand Dragon was Jane's father. He was the Dragon's lawyer.

Without Granny, Mamma, Judy, Cousin Sissy and Jane, there was no one who would understand. All the tears that had not poured from my eyes since Granny died, found mates with whom to share their journey over my eyelids, down my cheeks, uniting under my chin. They finally found rest, pooling in the sink made after I scooted down and layed my head on the pillow. The tears became a monsoon that seemed to last for hours. Through convulsing sobs, came the concerned thought, *Thank goodness my children are asleep and don't have to witness all this.*

The next morning, I awakened just as daylight began. I said my morning prayers, then "Well Robin ol' girl, you know whatcha gots ta do." So I tightly squeezed my right hand and whispered, "Well Lord, here we go for the 'umpteenth' time. Just me and You." With that I popped out of bed, cleaned my room and by the time I heard the first, "Maaaaaa," breakfast was on the table. For the first time in a while, I started my children's day by pouncing on their bed and slurping their faces rather than them jumping on mine. That morning I also experienced a feeling I knew was "real love." My heart sang a delightful melody and I felt warm all over. Felt safe, too. Safe in knowing that I without a doubt, I loved and was truly loved in return. Real love made me dedicate my life to my children.

"I will make the best home any child ever had, even without a father. I will fill our home with so much love and joy. Ellie and Chris will have no doubt where they belong."

In that moment, Ellie and Chris became the driving force behind everything I did. I was loving and joyful, just for them. Knew I had to finish school and work hard at becoming a great teacher so they would know it could be done, even from the Projects.

Finally, school was over. I had the degree that would allow me to teach future teachers. Instead of attending the graduation ceremony, I stayed home and Ellie and Chris baked me a cake. They wanted me to lie down so they could serve me dinner in bed. I didn't miss marching to "Pomp and Circumstance." Our family was together and happily celebrating the start of a new phase and that's all that mattered. The cake was a little lopsided, but good.

▲ ▼ ► ◄

Quickly, I learned that teaching was not a profession in which you took off your cap and gown and were handed a contract. I was "the sub" in a lot of K-12 rooms before I got the call that gave me purpose for many years.

Though I wasn't exactly thrilled initially, I later thought that teaching at my first alma mater would be perfect. At a community college, I could help would-be teachers prepare a solid foundation. Maybe even recruit a few. An added bonus was that since the school had an "open door" policy, it would afford me the opportunity to inspire and encourage other women who, like me, were struggling to rear children alone and also "make something out of themselves."

Don't you just love that phrase? It is as if you are nothing now, but if you work real, real hard, you might become…what? Human?

In addition to maintaining a nurturing home for my children, my life expanded to include the guidance and support of students, most of whom were women. I spent every spare moment during the daytime, figuring out a better way to teach. My children steadily grew and were my joy at the end of a workday filled with challenges.

Had I known what "open door" demanded, perhaps I would have better prepared. I certainly would have prepared differently.

"Open door" meant that in a single class there might be students functioning from second-grade to university graduate levels. Some students had just fought for and won freedom from abusive spouses, spoons and needles, or other assorted psychological, mental and emotional baggage so heavy that the residual raucousness could easily "resuck" them. In many cases, it did.

Some students found it hard to focus long enough to summon past learnings. When they did, often not to any degree of usefulness. Students sat ready and eager to learn, but didn't know how, since past experiences had them stuck somewhere between "go-go," "rock and roll" and "down home blues."

Hoped especially that Marvin's ho' with the baby would come. For some reason I searched every face at the beginning of every semester, but she was never among them.

There were students, however, who were more learned than I. Many had attended or graduated from universities, but in their cases, academics had not been related in a way that made the theories and concepts useful in their daily lives the way education should. Some were simply seeking an escape from a boredom I had yet to know.

My students and I both taught and learned. I set requirements thought to make academics and its pursuits meaningful to them. They made me conscious of my strengths and weaknesses, while teaching me lessons in life I may have missed. Few things gave me more pleasure than seeing the light of understanding suddenly click "on" in students' eyes.

So focused was I on creating an academic space in which my students could feel they belonged that I paid no attention to campus politics. That oversight could have proved harmful, but when the spewing political venom settled, it proved just the opposite.

A number of the women in my classes were older than I and had made five times the bad decisions. I must share at least one story:

Beverly walked up to me at that year's graduation ceremony.

"I have heard about your class and plan to take it next semester."

In an exaggerated professional voice I replied, "Great, I'll look forward to seeing you sitting in the front row the very first day."

We both chuckled.

On the first day of class, there sat Beverly, too far along to abort, in the back row rather than the front.

At the time, I didn't know this was Beverly's ninth pregnancy and that she didn't really know where her other children were after the courts took them years before. She didn't really know or care who had fathered the babies she delivered two months after semester's end. She just wanted children.

When I visited Beverly in the hospital, I felt compelled to ask, "So what now? What do you intend to do?"

"I want to get a degree and teach like you."

I assured her it was possible, but wouldn't be easy considering the two new mouths she now had to feed.

A couple of months later while I was on the phone with Ellie, now a senior at a local boarding school, my doorbell rang. There stood Beverly with the widest grin.

"I'm ready."

I thought, *Ready for what,* but said, "That's good! Come on in!"

When we sat, Beverly told me she had left her babies in Illinois with her aunt who had agreed to keep them while she finished school. I was so torn between, *"How could a mother abandon her children like that"* and *"This woman has enough guts to make it!"* that for a while, I was speechless.

Beverly and I sat that day and created a plan that would allow her time with her children, while she completed coursework over the next three years.

Close to Beverly's graduation from the community college, I encouraged her to take her children and move into married housing on the campus of a

West Coast university to which she had been accepted. She kept me abreast of her progress and I gave her what guidance I could and a shoulder. Unfortunately, I accepted a summer position abroad, which prevented me from attending her graduation.

Wonder if Beverly has ever forgiven me for that?

Years of trying to reach students and sharing the trials of so many other women, depleted even my reserves. I was drained. Had been so busy giving, until I had neglected to open myself up to receive what I needed. Long before, I had stopped identifying safe, supportive places I could go to revive and heal.

After about a million, zillion games of Solitaire, I remembered.

School! That's where I belong. Wonder if it still has its old magic?

I shared my plans with my colleagues. *Silly me!* Actually thought they would be supportive. Instead, I heard....

"Miss Robin, when will you ever be satisfied?"

"What more do you want? You already have a big house (*only the three bedrooms needed*) and you're driving a new Mercedes (*purchased because at the time I needed a new car, a student needed to be inspired and shown that academics could result in street-valued materials*). Each time I see you, you are dressed sharper than the time before. What more do you want?"

One colleague even tried to convince me that I should focus on the end of my career. Told me the exact number of years I had to retirement. Only Granny's words fit that situation.

"Well I'll be!"

I honestly thought people for whom education was their life and livelihood would encourage additional schooling and be happy about my pursuit. How could they not? When I encountered a former student in the library who had just been accepted into a doctoral program, I was a "happy camper." But were my colleagues?

"Noooooo!"

Why didn't I see that? Why didn't I also see that eventually my reward for helping other women would be the linking of my name with the word "lesbian" in gossip. The "real" lesbians know better. Okay, so my socializing with known lesbians confirms the gossip.

Later for them! Let them think what ever they want. Whatever they think, I will fraternize with anybody I choose. I see they're not true friends, anyway.

My colleagues more than anyone, even love for my children, sent me running back to school where I could at least breathe freely and feel safe.

Hallelujah!   Hallelujah!

PART IV

DR. T

▲ ▶ ◀ ▼

Finally! Clear, refreshing, logical thoughts! Being a student is marvelous.

Listening to the lecture, I felt that familiar, warm fit. Gradually, my relaxed mind surfaced and I got a glimpse of my old self; the self that is energetic, enthusiastic, cheerful and just plain fun.

This is exactly what I needed! Exactly where I need to be! Where I want to be!

My creativity increased. I thought of new ways to boost my students' understanding and use of academics. I was approaching bliss for the first time in years. But as usual in life, that soon changed.

After my first semester of classes, I applied for admission to the Doctoral Program. Went into the graduate office smiling and feeling good, came out knowing I was in for a very rough ride on a long journey.

My journey began with my application.

"For what college," the secretary asked.

"Liberal Arts."

"To which Department are you applying?"

When I answered, Becky stood up and stared at me…oddly. Gave me a look I couldn't quite read, because it was countered by her facial expression. Her eyes said, "I am genuinely concerned," but the raised eyebrows, fixed jaw and stiff, slight smile said the opposite.

Why would anybody who looks as if she has been pulled from underneath a bed and shaken out a few minutes before I walked into the office be concerned about me, rather than herself? I'd better pay attention to what the rest of her is saying.

I decided that Becky was simply an efficient "worker bee." Physical attractiveness and grooming were not considerations for her position. It was her voice that consistently reeked of compassion and bade me trust her.

After hearing the program for which I was applying, Becky looked me straight in the eyes, while saying, "You know they'll turn you down, don't you?"

"No, I don't. Why would they?"

She didn't answer.

I couldn't imagine why I would not be admitted, since according to the University catalog, I more than qualified. Besides, I had received my Masters from that same Department.

Before long, I understood Becky's look, though. It yelled, "Poor fool!"

"Let's send the application anyhow," I quipped. "We don't know what will happen. Maybe this will be the magic time."

She did.

They did.

Comments: Have not completed Masters in proposed major.

After reading the rejection reply, *take this to Becky* was my first thought. I took the letter to her the next day.

"What does this <u>really</u> mean? Why did they reject my application?"

Becky attempted an explanation, but was so uncomfortable with her effort that she dropped what she held in her hands, twice. She stammered and fidgeted. Watching her, threw me back to my Shetland days which made the real answer clear.

I felt sorry for Becky, in a way. After all, University policies were not hers to make. Though I didn't know where else to go, decided to leave her to regain her composure. Just as I turned to walk away the words, "You really want this don't you" shocked my ears.

"Yes I do," I yelled emphatically.

"Okay, I hear you. Don't tell anybody I told you, but this is what you might try: Take and pass a class from each of the professors in the Department with "B" or better. Then, reapply."

Though it was such a simple strategy, having been resucked into a state of confusion, I would never have thought of it.

In the next year, I followed Becky's advice almost to the letter. Took and passed thirty credits taught by all but one professor in the Department, Dr. Openheim. I didn't take his class because I thought him too weird, in looks, voice and mannerisms.

When Becky saw me walk through the door that next year, her smile was so broad, it made me smile. I reapplied. Then she suggested one more thing.

"After you receive your acceptance letter, you will need to petition to have the credits from all the classes you've taken, brought into your degree program."

Still smiling, Becky handed me the petition forms.

So confident was I that I would receive a "Welcome" reply, I happily awaited the Department's response. "But, noooooooo!" The rejection comments read, "Insufficient GPA."

"What? There must be something wrong. My GPA is way higher than what the University catalog says is required."

Hummmmm. Should I take this to Becky or where?

When I walked into the office to inquire, the Department Chair's body tightened. He began to fidget just the way Becky had that day.

"I received this form with 'insufficient GPA' listed as the explanation for my being denied acceptance into the Doctoral Program. Perhaps there has been a mistake."

Dr. Gaddis looked in my direction, but stared clear through me out into space. Even when he spoke, his eyes never made contact with mine. It was as if I was not sitting right in front of him. I hadn't seen that look in so long, I had almost forgotten it.

The last time I had seen "the look" was when I interviewed in answer to an ad in the Shetland Ledger for a receptionist position. The interviewer gave me "the look" and right then I knew I would never hear from her. Sure enough, when I walked into my dentist's office, a pretty, young White girl looked up and said, "Ya'll got an appointment?" There was nobody with me, so the question went unanswered.

Who in the hell is 'y'all?'

"The GPA required by the University and the one required by the Department are different, Miss Talbin," Dr. Gaddis said, now alternating his gaze between empty space and his office window. "We have our own."

Mine was still higher.

"What I recommend is that you take a few undergraduate courses, get A's in them, then reapply."

If you wonder why he called me Miss Talbin, I took back the name during my divorce. Couldn't stand being called Mrs. Gibson without truly being. Plus, I didn't want daily reminders of what should have been.

The combination of "the look" and Dr. G's recommendation commanded a *Robin ol' girl, position yourself for fight*. My mind flipped from its usual conciliatory to an armored mode that catapulted my body into creative animation.

My first act was asking Dr. G if I could inspect my academic file.

"…Maybe something has been overlooked."

Sure enough, there had been an oversight.

"My summer courses have been posted to my transcript without grades, Sir. Does that lower my GPA?"

"You took classes during the summer? What were they? What grades did you get?"

Dr. G turned beet red and his skin slightly glistened, especially after what I told him was confirmed by the Department's records in the archival drawers to which he hastily went without saying a word to me. For the first time since I had entered his office, he met my gaze.

"Well Robin, you know I can't go against the decision of the Department. You will have to take at least three courses. Maybe, you can combine them into a directed study with Dr. Steiner."

"Who is Dr. Steiner? A new professor? Where is his office?"

I knew talking to Dr. G anymore would be a waste of time. Leaving his office, I did turn and ask if he would send me a letter explaining exactly what the Department required, since it was not what was posted. He did. I am sure he regrets doing that to this day.

Walking into Dr. Steiner's office, I handed him the copy of my transcript I had neatly tucked into my purse in case I needed information from it.

"The Department thinks I should take three undergraduate courses as a directed study supervised by you."

Dr. Steiner looked at my transcript and "Why are they doing that?" popped out of his mouth before he could catch it. I certainly understood how that could happen.

He is new, poor thing. They haven't gotten to him with directions regarding me, yet.

"Well, if that's what they want you to do. Here, fill out this form and tell me what you will do in your study."

I felt a little sorry for Dr. Steiner, because I knew he was in their palms and like me, had tough times ahead. He got plenty.

The tactics used to impede my degree pursuit became stock jokes between me and the "favoreds;" other doctoral students who were taken under wings and guided toward rewarding careers. Thankfully, the "favoreds" would report the Department's next move, often in the time it took them to find me after their meeting was over. In return, I critiqued their papers. Was I ever invited to a Department meeting like my fellows? Not only was I never invited, but each time I was close to completing my coursework, new requirements were reported from the meetings that meant I had more courses to take. Requirements were changed in a way that most often affected only me.

Over ten years, I received reports from four "favoreds." Never was I chosen or asked to do anything that would connect me to a career. Even when I published in an international journal, it was never suggested that I share my research at any conference or participate in any forum. The "favoreds" were not only invited, but coached.

Oh before I forget, let me tell you how I finally got accepted into the program. Here's the story:

My second denial came two days after I received the letter from the Chair stating the Department's requirements. By that time, the formerly all WASP, male Department had been infiltrated by...dah, dah, dah, dah!...a woman. A University reorganization had placed second in command, the woman who headed the area from which I had received my Masters.

"Call Dr. Lee," 'the voice' instructed as I was staring at the denial letter.

I thought, *Great idea*, and picked up the phone. Didn't know what I would say, but squeezed my right hand and out of my mouth flowed words to make the appointment. Thankfully, Dr. Lee had office hours the next day, or I may have cowered.

I felt strange going to talk with Dr. Lee that day, although I had spoken with her many, many times before. Had taken courses from her and worked on a project with her after graduation.

"Squeeze Robin ol' girl, squeeze," the voice commanded.

The courage I needed came. I opened the door, walked into Dr. Lee's office and sat in the first seat I saw. My insides started jiggling in double-time. Then, my mouth took over. I am so glad it knew what to say. The pace at which my mind raced prevented the formation of anything concrete.

"Sooooo Robin, why did you want to see me," Dr. Lee asked almost sarcastically.

I only remember saying, "There are some strange things happening and I need someone who can explain them to me." After that, my mind went completely blank. The next thing I recollect was something about the Chair's letter and then thanking Dr. Lee for her time.

I headed toward the door. As soon as my hand touched the doorknob....

"Robin!"

"Yes," turning expectantly.

"Do you really want in?"

"Yes!"

"Do you really, really want in?"

"Yes, I do!"

"Then, you're in."

That's all it took. I really mean, that-is-all-it-took. Six days later, I received my "Welcome" letter. Though I was a happy camper to be welcomed, I knew this was not a journey that would end in a comfortable home stay. By that time though, I was resigned to do what it took. I owed that much to Dr. Lee and Becky.

A whole lot of hand squeezing went on during those doctoral years. Sometimes, a squeeze for courage. Other times, to keep from acting on generatively recurring negative impulses. I knew I was really in trouble though, when the words "You have always felt secure in school. Now they are trying to f—k that up. You need to take a 57 and blow the hell out of all of them, or they will never stop sh---ng on niggahs" flashed like a neon sign, covering my entire mind all at once. It wasn't the message that alarmed me. I had felt like that many times. Knew I would never do anything so crazy. What really disturbed me was how cuss words and the "N" word had inserted themselves into a natural place in my mind's statements as though they really belonged.

"How dare you!"

As if in reply, I heard "the voice" say, "So stop with the pictures, admit you are angry and do something about it." As "the voice" continued speaking, the letters faded.

Maybe that's you talking back to me, huh? Did you finally find a way, after all these years? What if all thoughts are simply transmissions from other minds?

"Robin ol' girl, you need to stop concocting wild theories, listen and do something about your anger."

I listened.

"You would do well to consult the only professor of color assigned to the Department. Maybe he would be willing to guide you through this maze."

"The voice" probably used the word "assigned," because though he was a celebrated expert in his field, Dr. Dotson's presence in the Department was primarily on paper. He only taught one course in the Department, but that was enough to support University compliance for continued Governmental aide. Most of the time, Dr. Dotson was "on loan" to the Education Department where all of <u>us</u> were sent, professors and students alike. Our conversation shocked me:

Me: Dr. Dotson, I came to see you because I need to know
how to sanely and successfully get through the
Department's doctoral program. Can you help me?

Dr. D: The best advice I can give is that you apply to a program
at a different University.

Me: Why? Why should I travel miles to another university,
when this one is five minutes away from my job?

Dr. D: They will never let you graduate, you know.

Hearing Becky's words paraphrased, startled me, but for some reason, energized me. Maybe it was my already armored mind, but I suddenly felt I had the strength of Superman.

"I am not going anywhere! They will grant me a degree from this university and that's that," I whispered through clenched teeth as soon as I closed Dr. Dotson's door.

I tightly buckled my mind's armor hoping it would protect me while I jostled or whatever I had to do to win my degree. I even rejected my "special invitation" to transfer to the much maligned and under funded College of Education.

Can you believe this of a university plopped down in the heart of Northern urbana? We <u>are</u> near the end of the 20^{th,} not the 18th century, aren't we?

My "special invitation" had come from my first advisor. Had four, one for each change in requirements.

I went to the advisor's office, to get his signature on a registration form. Upon my arrival, I could see he was in conference. His door was open. The student (White) was comfortably seated. I waited in the hallway as my advisor's gesture indicated. When it was my turn, I stooped to gather my bags. Before I could stand up, the advisor whisked past and said, "Follow me," seemingly as an afterthought.

With my file underarm, he walked swiftly down the hallway. I followed, feeling the way I know a child must feel being taken to the principal's office for being bad. By the time we sat down in the reception office, I knew I had really been taken to the office for being "Black."

Well, at least they both begin with the letter "b!"

My advisor opened the file and gave me my "special invitation" without ever looking up. When he finished, all I thought was, *Well I'll be!*

I am sure you understand the kinds of difficulties I had being the only Black doctoral student in that Department, so I won't bore you with the zillion other debasing scenarios over all those years.

I know what! Maybe one day, I should publish a guidebook entitled, "How to Get a Ph.D. from a European Centered University Though Black." Or should I end the title with, "...and Remain Ethnically Sane" to be politically correct?

I can see it now. Groups of bewildered and distraught doctoral students of color huddled in discussion.

Do you think this will work here at ------ U?

Perhaps this would resolve my problem with Dr. ---------.

I wish you could help me write it.

▶ ◀ ▼ ▲

"Broken, bloody, but unbowed," I stayed in my position at the Community College after graduation. Just didn't have the energy or mental fortitude to do anything else. Needed to heal after years of walking around in quiet panic. Years of feeling the resigned destiny of a chicken with strong hands wrapped firmly around its neck. Knowing that at any second, on a whelm, my head could be severed and hurled into eternity.

One thing that gave those years value though, were the Black students who called to tell me they had been admitted to the Department's graduate program. They thanked me for "sticking it out" so they could enjoy their present status. You know what? They didn't even get the "special invitation." Most of the old-guard professors from whom I had taken classes, retired when the rules changed that meant people of color must have an equal chance at admission.

A few weeks into my work semester that year, I noticed a difference in the classroom environment. I became increasingly aware that communicating with students was more difficult than usual.

Have students changed right before my eyes? Have I been so focused on my studies that I forgot what students are really like? Have I changed in some negative way? Is college instructor no longer my calling? What could it be that's making the exchange of information with students so difficult?

Thought maybe it would help to change the examples I used during my lectures.

Maybe I need to change to a more individualized teaching method like I would do with elementary students. Maybe my colleagues have some good suggestions. Maybe I need to...." On and on and on my thoughts raged, trying to concoct a workable solution.

No matter what I did, many of my students simply were not able to demonstrate the concepts discussed. Nothing seemed to help. There was definitely something wrong and I didn't know what. But I would soon find out.

Sitting in the cafeteria one day I saw Tommy, a counselor, walk through the doors. He was his usual charming, "dapper," aloof self. Had a way that seemed to drive women out of their minds. Sometimes they were even crazy enough to fall for him, despite their knowing his devious, womanizing ways. I probably didn't fall for his "aura fantazia" because I was a close friend of one of the "crazy" ones. (Don't worry, I told her what a lunatic she was many, many times.)

When Tommy saw me, he waved and indicated he would join me later. I watched as the food server heaped onto his plate, two big pieces of smothered chicken and topped them with lots of onions and gravy. All he did was point twice and smile. Valley girl talk came to mind when I saw who his server was.

Like girrlll, I gave Mr. Tommy two <u>big</u> ol' pieces of chicken and piled on the onions and gravy when he came through my line...with his f-i-n-e self.

Many people would think "valley girl" a very pretty woman. Marsha was tall and slim with very long hair that she usually wore in one or two ponytails. She was a Culinary Arts student who had overcome much to get to stand behind the lunch counter.

Marsha had spent most of her teen years in "Juvy." She ran away, drank, smoked and drugged with her friends, despite how often her mother prayed over her and dragged her to church. She never had Granny's "strap in the sky" constricting her like I did.

One night, Marsha and her friends stole a car and being high from the chosen substance(s) of the night, rammed it into the back of another car in which was a family returning home after the movies. The whole family died when their car went off the road, flipped down an embankment and into a ravine. The ravine was shallow enough for them to have survived had they gotten help immediately, but Marsha and her friends "got outta there" as fast as they could. They knew the consequences of their carelessness and were scared. Though the incident happened over 20 years before, Marsha had never forgotten.

Rememberings sunk Marsha into deep depression for years. She tried anesthetizing with alcohol. Didn't work. Went to heavier drugs. "Thanks to the missionaries, drugs never took over," she told me. But an overdose did get her to a helpful therapist who asked the right questions. Her responses were self-enlightening and began her journey toward long-overdue changes. Enrolling in school was one of them.

Even after all this time, Marsha was still unable to get behind the wheel of a car. She spoke in a squeally, soft voice as if she was frightened of what someone would do if they heard her clearly. If there was a man nearby that she liked though, Marsha was loud. Too loud.

It was Marsha's loud voice that sounded like a bad imitation of a valley girl. What she said, was usually truthful and insightful. In the few conversations I had had with her, I came away with a deeper respect for what and how much humans can overcome.

As Tommy walked toward me, he thought I was smiling at him. But I was really trying not to laugh at what I knew Marsha was saying in her mind as she looked in his direction.

Tommy sat and sang, "Congratulations to you, congratulations to you. Congratulations, congratulations...." We ate and caught up. The children, his wife, Ph.D. war stories. Then he told me.

"Robin, I am so glad you're finally finished with school and back with us full time. I've needed someone into whose class I could send the increased number of special needs students we're getting these days. I know you will at least <u>try</u> to teach them. The others won't keep them. Sometimes they send them back to my office with a dismissal note the first day."

I knew there was something different! Now I know what!

Want to hear an open-door-special-needs story? Don't say "no." Just listen. By now, you know I have to tell these side-stories every once in a while. Here goes:

One day when I walked into my classroom, I saw sets of the number six all over the blackboard. Sixes had been written with both the points and sides of chalk in every imaginable direction. Sixes in sets of threes leaned to the left and to the right. Some were upside down, while others were right side up. Sets fanned out connected at their tops, others connected at bottoms. There were big ones and little ones with all available board space filled.

Though there were over thirty students in the room, not a sound was heard when I walked in. I looked at the board, then sat at my desk and thought, *Oooooookay. How do I respond to this?* To the class I said, "I'm going to get a drink of water and by the time I return, I want the "artist" who filled the board to have retired this masterpiece. In other words, erase the board!" By the time I returned, someone had complied.

I did nothing to try and identify the artist. But right in the middle of one student's verbal report, a young man who had before that day shown much promise, jumped up and ran across the room. The door slammed so loud that some of the students jumped. Again I thought, *Oooooookay.* Might have said it aloud. But one thing was clear: I had to confront the student or risk a repeat.

I decided to wait outside of the classroom for my impending encounter. To do or say what, I did not know. On my way out, Jasper and my hands must have touched the doorknob simultaneously. I walked through, truncating his advance.

"What's wrong?"

"Nothing, what do you mean, Dr. Talbin."

"I know you must have had an emergency to disrupt the class that way."

You will never guess what he said.

"Dr. Talbin, you don't understand. You see, I am a doctor, too! And, whenever I hear ill, I have to operate."

Ooooookay. Well I'll be. How in hell do you respond to something this bazaar, Miss Robin?

Jasper told me he had to leave the class right then, because "the voice" told him to leave. "The voice" had also told him to write the sixes.

Remember I said that I learned valuable life-lessons from students? This was one of them. You know that my number and letter pictures had been replaced by "the voice," right? Well, Jasper taught me not to ever do anything dictated by "the voice," without questioning the rationality of the action. The notion, "When in doubt, do (say) nothing" is one I embrace to this very day, thanks to my open-door, special-needs student.

That year, the phrase "special needs" had taken on a new meaning, one that made me eagerly await semester's end. Being a professional helper, I was suffering "burnout," the all-too-familiar energy imbalance (more going out than coming in). I looked forward to the summer more than ever as a time for me to refresh and renew. I envied bears that had been all curled up snuggly for their winter's nap. At the time, however, I didn't know that one of my friends and colleagues was suffering, too.

◀▲▶▼

I had met Sid the first year I started teaching at the college. We tried romance. Didn't work. Decided to "just be friends." Most who saw us thought we were in love, judging by the way we acted whenever we were together. People could see that we shared something special. We knew it, too. Didn't know what to call it, but didn't want to call it love. It was just something special we shared.

Sid was the kind of professional who kept "street" in his life. He had grown up in the Projects and still hung with his "buds from the 'hood." Most of Sid's buds had also gotten degrees and "good jobs." Could have said "professional positions," but Sid and his buds thought of their work only as jobs. They never let go of their truth that "on a whelm, our good jobs can be snatched away."

"You should be more secure than this if you have a professional position, shouldn't you," one of them asked one day.

Sid and his friends kept each other "grounded and real." Often reminding each other that being Black, degreed, and professional only meant that you could see "the promise land," not that you would ever reach it. This they knew was especially true if the presence of a Black was unnecessary for the company's almighty "bottom line." Report for work in the morning to cluelessly find your entire Department dissolved. They knew someone to whom this had happened.

"Poor brother. Poor stupid brother for thinking he had it made. Had cut himself off from his 'peeps,' too."

Years passed before I actually met Sid's buds. They laughingly embraced me.

"We have heard Sid talk about you for years. We thought he made you up. You <u>are</u> real, huh?"

I was immediately brought into the group and made to feel at home. With them, I could just…"Be." No matter what I said or did, they would treat me with loving respect. It also helped that by that time, I was willing to enjoy "deep" conversations with them while under the influence. That summer, my motto became: Relax! Release! Escape! The farther under we were, the more articulate and profound our discussions. The world had not a single problem we couldn't solve. Those we chose not to, we laughed at.

"Ain't worth the energy. N-E-X-T!" (Ha! Ha! Ha!)

After a while, we organized and creatively (*Ha!*) called ourselves "Group." At any moment I could pick up the phone and hear, "You coming to Group Friday?" We invited others to join and a few did.

I had found a family.

Initially, Group did for me what a support group should, helped me to cope. I went into Group like a wounded bird unable to lift its wings, too weighted down with…life. I shared my pains with other recovering woundeds and somehow, we all left better able to fly. I wouldn't soar after every meeting, but was at least able to flap and hover.

There was nothing excluded from discussion at Group. When a White colleague took research I had been compiling for years and published under his name only, I went to Group. When helping had drained me dry, I went to Group. When I acquired an original Mother Goose book, I took the poem "Ten Little Niggers" to Group. In Group I was even able to share those times when my heart was open and bleeding "'cause my baby done, done me wrong." Group members probably thought I dropped out because I got bored with them. "But, noooooo!" It's just that I finally agreed with "the voice's" council.

"If you don't stop it, you're gonna get hooked!"

After Group, I consulted a professional. Prayed…a lot! Consoled myself with my on-going dream of one-day living in Africa surrounded by beautiful, rich and powerful people my same color. I continually longed to be swallowed whole into African blackness, travel peacefully to a softly lined cultural belly containing all the juices I needed to act fearlessly, unencumbered by race.

I also rediscovered books. I read and read and read and....

► ▲ ◄ ▼

"If you're unhappy where you are, leave," repeated the novel's heroine. I read and reread the story until I understood Canata through and through. Canata knew where she belonged: wherever she was comfortable and free enough to express her true self. She lived light, owning few material trappings so she could move if and when it was time.

Wherever Canata went, she was never without her hisses. She thought the three small bird carvings were her "direct link to the voice of the Almighty."

"What other creatures have the Almighty made free to soar the heavens with few concerns?"

Carved from mahogany, each bird was uniquely positioned. One was in flight with wings at full expanse as if cruising majestically in proprietal space. Another hiss sat on a tree stump that was obvious leavings of age and rot, perched with wings lifted slightly as if still wondering, "should I fly or just rest here a while longer?" The third bird was sitting on a stump that seemed to have been carved by man in pursuit of sawmill bounty. With wings tucked, it sat peacefully as if awaiting a disturbing, "Shoo!"

Whenever Canata couldn't make a decision (because life had gotten just plain crazy), she sat on her bed, dropped her hisses into a bag, shook them, and after closing her eyes and whispering a prayer for guidance, poured them out. Whichever bird fell closest to where she sat, determined her next move. Sitting bird, stay. Bird in flight, go. Mid, stay but change mindset and behavior. The latter took the greatest effort.

Canata loved people with a love they could feel. Loving them didn't mean she felt compelled to try and save them. She saw no value in sympathizing or commiserating.

"Each person is a whole. Strong and capable of living his own life without me, beyond a helpful word or two; a helpful deed or two," she'd say. Canata felt that to see people otherwise, honored weakness in the human chain.

"We are all bound together. A weakness in one means a weakness in all. I would rather spend my time focused on our strengths."

Whenever anyone came to dump their pain, Canata would listen attentively, then inspiringly give the same advice: "If you're unhappy where you are, leave." Sometimes, she would use an advisory tone, other times simply ask.

"Are you unhappy where you are? Then why don't you leave?"

Canata lived what she spoke. When she felt definite unrest or discontent, everything stopped and she took "quiet time" to try and move toward those thoughts, behaviors and attitudes she knew would bring ease. *(Aha! That's what I should have done this summer!)* If that didn't work after repeated tries, there were always her hisses.

"Most times, the move from discontentment to peace simply takes a change of head."

I had at last found my "shero." Found her at a time when I believed in little and trusted even less. Here was a woman who, unlike me, lived life in a way that kept her mind clear. She knew she could generally trust its dictates. If not, prayer and her hisses would guide her.

Like characters in the book, I started going to Canata to "dump." Over and over in a lyrical refrain, she repeated her advice mantra. Gradually, I made it my mantra, too.

"I am unhappy here. I know I need to leave, but where can I go? Back to Shetland?"

My decision to leave, stirred a before unseen hornet's nest. My friends acted as if they thought I had gone insane. They buzzed around me itemizing every possible error of my decision.

"How can you leave a house you have worked so hard to decorate, just when it is picture perfect?"

"You are leaving your good job...for what?"

Even Sid, on whom I had always been able to count for support, thought I needed to "wake up." With each encounter, he grew more and more vicious during our exchanges. I guess those were his attempts to jolt me awake.

When I called Ellie and Chris, they said in their I-think-you-are-just-in-crisis-and-need-support voices, "Okay Mom. If that's what you think best. How can we help you?" When my time of departure grew near, Ellie came home under the guise of helping me pack and seeing me off. I always knew she and Chris had talked and decided that one of them should come to see "what is really going on with Mom."

Ellie watched my every move like a hawk assessing its prey. She made me feel so uncomfortable that twice I had to firmly will myself not to yell out, "stop it!"

The "coup d'etat" (a word that would triple in meaning later) was planned during a surprise bon voyage party. Family, friends, mentees and even old loves came. Jeff wasn't there, because not accepting the counsel of his "voice," he had joined the fix-me-and-nothing-else-matters club many years before, taking away the best "do it" in the world. (Well, in my world anyhow.) I doubt if he would have come even if Ellie had invited him when she visited.

Are the old loves here to show support, or to lay eyes on the woman they have always thought most likely to go mad, who finally has?

The party was in a conference room of a five-star hotel. Chris flew in for the occasion. We all laughed, ate, drank and danced until we were soaked, then laughed some more. Periodically, Ellie reminded me, "See Mom, you are loved and needed right here. What if you get there and things are not the way you think. What if that is really nowhere you can live?"

Huh, does she think I am really crazy? Why is she acting as if she doesn't know that my contract is only for six months?

I will have to admit that at the beginning of the night, I started rethinking my decision. But as the night rolled on, Canata came to me in her most comforting voice, "Can you honestly say you will be happy here?"

"No!"

"Then why don't you...."

Like magic, my mind was clear, but uneasiness started to brew.

They want me to stay so I can continue to serve and nurture them! Can't they see I am all dry? Can't they see that if I stay here, I will surely die?

At home in bed, I had to pray for my mind to quiet and that sleep would overtake me. Finally, it did.

When my eyes opened, I woke stronger in my resolve, thanking Canata. Then, I looked out of my window and saw a bird's nest in the corner of my awning. The baby birds sat inside, chirping vigorously as their mother tried to evenly distribute her supply. I watched keenly as she flew back and forth, back and forth. Each time she returned, her chickees chirped just as vigorously and mouths stretched just as widely as before.

How many trips will she need to make? How long before it's enough?

The answer to my thought was obvious. Enough would not be enough until the chickees could soar the heavens solo and gather their own supply. Ellie and

Chris had been soaring for a while. My friends could certainly solo. Just I, still sat perched with weighted wings only partially extended.

It is *time for me to extend my wings and at least <u>try</u> to soar. I need to express who I am, instead of who I need to be for others. I-t i-s t-i-m-e!*

I could almost hear Canata breathe a sigh.

Here I come!   Mother, here I come!

PART V

ROBIN MARIE TALBIN

(FINALLY) GOES TO AFRICA

▼ ◄ ► ▲

Sitting in the airport, I couldn't think clearly for the storm of questions flooding my mind. With uncontrollable quickness, one question replaced the other as if my brain was in an answer-seeking hurricane.

Have I gone mad? I mean, have I really gone mad? Do I have to go so far to truly feel at home? If I want to go home, shouldn't I be on my way to Shetland where I was born? What if in life there is no such place like what I've been seeking? Does the place where I can leave the challenges and miseries of the world behind and bask only in what makes me feel whole really exist?

A mental spanking substituted for answers.

Robin Marie Talbin, why do you always have to take things to the extreme? Again, you're just being a "drama queen!" You need to get yourself together and stop being so selfish.

Despite my bantering brain, I still felt a guarded excitement. For the first time I was doing something for nobody else, but me. If that was selfish…Oh well. I was excited to finally be fulfilling the dream that had mushroomed ever since I first thoughtfully studied the African scene in the picture hanging over Granny's mantle. National Geographics cinched it. I had to live in Africa, or my life would never be complete.

I sung, *"I'm going to Africa, I am go-ing to A-fri-ca,"* over and over in my mind to tunes from nursery rhymes to rumba. Envisioned myself dancing to the rhythms while I sung. When my flight was called, I excitedly rushed to stand near the ticket taker so I would be first in my section to board.

Settled in my seat, I imagined all the colorfully dressed, dark faces that would greet me when I landed. Felt them warmly embracing their prodigal daughter/sister, welcoming her home.

The magazine I took from the seat pocket showed exactly what I was thinking. Page after page, glossy prints of African males dressed in flowing robes draped with indigenous riches paraded as I flipped. Some stood in front of huts happily displaying gold and wooden treasures of which they were now the trusted protectors. African women were also pictured, adorned with rich ivory, alabaster and wooden bobbles and beads creatively carved, etched, and scored. They bore their breasts unashamedly. Dark, dark skin and white, white teeth gleamed in bright sunlight.

The males reminded me of Sam. The women reminded me of what might have been with Sam, a thought that after all the years, still surged warmth from my head to my toes.

It has been so long since I have even thought about Sam. Wonder if he ever thinks about me? While I'm over there, I think I'll visit his Country and find out. Wonder if he will recognize me, or I him? Would he even want to see me after the way we ended? Surely after over forty years, he would not still be holding a grudge, if he ever felt he had one.

Thoughts of Sam tapered into a doze. The crackle of the magazine falling to the floor, startled me awake. When I reached down and picked it up, I looked at the opened page and wondered.

How can people in Africa be happy living in mud huts? With all their riches, why don't they build themselves comfortable homes? They could build state-of-the-art schools for their children, too. Have fine, fine clothes and cars. Why don't they? Without any of that, they are always joyful. How can that be?

There they stood in what looked to me like dire poverty with wide, happy grins. I knew I had to know the secret of that kind of joy.

▼ ◄ ▲ ▶

The plane landed. Out of the window, I saw a most disturbing site. Soldiers were watching every movement with their berets tilted and guns cocked at ready. My insides shuttered. Thought about Ellie's warnings and wondered just how closely my dreams and this reality <u>would</u> fit. I had been warned that the soldiers would be standing guard, but knowing didn't lessen the disturbance I felt actually seeing them. Didn't expect so many.

What else will I find in this mysterious land? Can I ever be content in a place so heavily guarded?

Are there any green leopards? I have never seen shrubbery, trees or other greenery with leopard spots, I thought looking at the soldiers' khaki, beige and green camouflage uniforms.

Suddenly, one of the soldiers stared straight into my eyes and shouted, "marchez vite, marchez vite" in a voice that chilled my insides. I turned and walked quickly as he had commanded. Shifting my gaze, I saw a man holding a VentuFar, Inc. sign with my name on it and breathed a noticeable sigh.

"Dr. Talbin?"

"Yes, yes!

"I will take you to our jeep and come back. By that time, your luggage should be up."

"Oh, thank you. That long trip took more out of me than I expected."

VentuFar was the agency that had arranged my trip. They guaranteed I would live in a "real" African village with a "real" African family. No frills.

The agency had provided months of language and cross-cultural training to prepare me. Though I looked forward to a new lifestyle, I was not prepared for one that resembled what I had known only in basic sensory ways. Little did I know that though I would still be able to see, hear, feel and taste, everything else would be different. Didn't expect my sense of smell to be so violently attacked, either.

The second I walked out of the airport, a jolting odor blasted my nose and immediately sent my stomach into convulsions. I rushed toward the jeep ahead of the agent. Thought if I made it, my siege would somehow be quelled. My stomach knotted, increasing the convulsions to a zillion summersaults per minute. The rapidly mounting queasiness was soon joined by an uncontrollable lip quiver. I could barely walk. The agent waiting by the jeep, began running toward me holding a piece of gauze with which he covered my nose. Whatever soaked the gauze, eased the convulsive feelings immediately.

By the time the jeep wheels rolled, I was calm enough to again question the rationality of my journey.

Will Mother Africa provide the kind of warmth and contentment I always thought She would? She is called "Mother" for that reason, isn't She? Will those I meet truly embrace me and welcome me as their American daughter/sister? I heard rumors that Africans scorn Black Americans. What if that's true?

Robin, Robin ol' girl, you've got to stop obsessing. Look out of the window and enjoy the scenery! Maybe that will keep your mind and stomach calm. Afterall, it's too late now. What ever happens, you'll just have to deal with it.

"Are there always so many soldiers at the airport?"

"Not only at the airport, Dr. Talbin. Did you forget we are under military rule? But there is no reason to be frightened. Your papers are in order."

Warily, I settled back in a position that gave me the best view of the scenery.

"Now I understand Paul Simon's musical plea to save the rainforest. I liked his songs, but never really understood what they meant."

"Is Paul Simon a musician or singer?"

"Oh I forgot you may not know him. He's a famous singer who campaigned to save the rainforest."

"I have heard of his campaign. Just didn't remember his name."

Never did I expect to ride for miles and miles in the rainforest seeing so little vegetation. Every once in a while one or two trees appeared on an otherwise flat and empty horizon. They were obviously leftovers. I was appalled that man would do such a thing, especially since the rainforest is so vital to the world's ecosystem.

Did they even question what destroying the rainforest would mean to human life? Did they even care? Probably not. It was all about money!

I understand you now, Paul, I thought, looking toward the sky as though my upward gaze united me with him and his cause.

A sudden jolt interrupted my thoughts. The jeep had turned onto an unpaved road. The uneasiness I was trying to ignore, leaped headlong into dread. I countered with thoughts of home.

Wonder what Chris and Ellie are doing? Let's see. It's 2:00 o'clock there now. In one hour, I would be leaving work.

Where are you Miss Hanan? Why didn't you come with me? What will I do when I need somebody to talk to? Somebody to "run things by?"

There would be no old friend for me to call. Realizing that, my feeling of loneliness grew heavier than it had been the day I realized I couldn't count on Judy and Mamma for support. Then, at least I had Ellie and Chris to comfort me, though they could not remove the ball of emptiness I carried in my heart until my surprise visit the night before my graduation.

Mamma and Judy will just look at this announcement and toss it aside. But I have to send it. I have to do what is right.

I was irritated when I heard the doorbell ring that night. Thought I would have to get up and entertain.

"Who is it Chris?"

"It's Grandma and Auntee Judy."

I thought, *Oh, what now,* never imagining they would remember or even want to celebrate my success. As much as the children, Mamma and Judy made my night. They came into the bedroom with a "You did it!" song. Then, they handed me a bag. I peeked inside and excitedly pulled out a beautiful maroon, leather briefcase.

Wow!

Mamma and Judy hugged me repeatedly and told me how proud they were of me. They assured me they would come early to the graduation ceremony.

"With bells on," Judy added.

By the time they left, the long-opened hole in my heart was nearly filled.

I am happy that I didn't have to come way over here with my heart still open and hurting. Thank you Mamma! Thank you Judy!

Wonder why I couldn't get <u>anybody</u> to come with me? I know they have heard people say, "Black people come from Africa." Why weren't they at least a little curious to know what there ancester's original home is like? I wonder...Do <u>you</u> want to know?

Without warning, my whole body shook. Probably from the feeling of impending doom. Sweat poured so fast that rapid dabbings and repeated long wipes could not keep my blouse from getting soaked. Though wet, I still felt like tumbleweed, void of color and life, blowing aimlessly down that hot, dusty African road. Toward what? I did not know.

I must have had a strange look on my face, or something. The agent began reassuring me.

"Dr. Talbin, there is a lot of America in Africa, you know. Right now we are passing a village where there's a big hospital. See the white block building? It was built and is run by one of the American churches. I forget which one. You might want to come visit it sometime."

The agent also assured me that the by-road leading directly to Alemokon was not far. And, that our now two-hour ride would soon be over. As we rolled along, he pointed out other sites in which he thought I might have interest: the Peace Corps office, the radio station with its tall tower, shopping areas where I could get the greatest value and villages where jewelry artisans sold their creations on market day.

Did someone tell him how much time and money I spend shopping? That's one addiction I hope this trip will cure.

Initially I was grateful for all of the information, but the agent talked on and on for so long that I stopped listening and refocused on the view.

"Bump! Bumpity! Bump! Thud!

We were off the main road and on the by-road to Alemokon, the village where I would live.

The agent, who was driving, had to slow the jeep to give the wheels' shocks and springs time for expansion down into the ruts and gullies left by weeks of hard, pouring rain. Then, retraction back to road level. The jeep vigorously rocked as it rolled.

Suddenly we were completely swallowed by what I had expected of a rainforest. On both sides, we were surrounded by grass taller than Jabar, or any other basketball player, standing on Magic's shoulders. The grass was so thick that I could only see the first row of shoots. A blanket of red dust covered the grass's roots for what must have measured five feet or more high. It was a marked contrast to the deep green wave of the grass's undusted tops.

The grass was steadily fanned by wind from the moving jeep efficaciously splitting the air. Looking out of both the front and back windows, all I saw were grassy waves.

Now I know how it must look to Barry standing center court, football in hand, watching sections of fans in coordinated sequence, stand up, raise and lower their arms, then sit until it's their section's turn again.

I had to lie down on the seat and look out of the back window to get the full effect. When I did, my attention was snatched by the tops of trees looming high over the grass. The unusually shaped tree branches seemed to issue a come-at-your-own-risk dare.

"I accept your dare! I will handle everything you offer! I have waited a long, long time for this and have sacrificed much. No matter what, I won't turn back now," I whispered making sure the sounds were covered by engine noise.

For what felt like hours (but was probably only a half), we bumped along. Increasingly, the jeep's wheels expanded and retracted, dropped and pulled. I had read about the mudslides and washouts during the long rainy season. Was happy I missed it. Didn't want to experience getting stranded in a village the way I had been warned could happen.

I hope the short rainy season won't be too bad.

Suddenly, through an unexpected break in the thickness. I saw a short, narrow bridge. Heard sounds of life. Talk. Laughter.

"Taking their turn in the marigot," the agent said.

On one side of the bridge, naked children romped or bobbed up and down in the stream of water. Some were soapy from head to toe, some not. Some splashing while others just stood, watched and giggled. All were having fun cooling their bodies in the austere heat of the day.

On the other side of the bridge, women were washing dishes in that same stream. Only one of the women looked up as we slowly passed overhead. And, she only glanced.

Can't they see that that water is too dirty for dishes? What about the germs from the children's bodies? Or, animals that may have crossed upstream?

The jeep's motor made a loud grinding noise, drawing my attention away from the bathers and washers. We were mounting a steep hill.

"Dr. Talbin, get ready. Alemokon is just around the bend."

Hearing that, my body tightened with anticipation. A final engine grind turned us into the yard of a little church.

How did these villagers get the special paint to stain those window panes? I thought. *Maybe somebody brought it in from the City on market day. How in the world do they keep the church so white when everything else around is dusty red or gray? Is it painted every month? Every week? How long and how many hands did it take to carve the scenes in those wooden mahogany doors? Beautiful! Granny would be happy to see that Africans keep their church so neat.*

My thoughts changed when I saw through the jeep's windshield the large, roofed concrete block toward which we were heading. A cluster of dark faces stood waiting. It was the colorful scene I had often imagined.

The jeep slowed to a stop. Door opened. We descended into outstretched arms that gave long, robust hugs. Then three kissing taps, alternating cheeks.

"Akwaba! Akwaba! Bon arrive! Bonne arrivee!"

"Merci! Merci," the agents and I said in syncopated unison.

Just as I was beginning to relax a bit from the warmth of my welcome, out of the crowd stepped a man with a better-to-eat-you-my-dear grin. He was my host father.

Do all fathers grin at there daughters like that? Hummmm.

In broken French, my host introduced himself. With four missing front teeth (I counted every space), his grin though meant to be a happy, welcoming one I am sure, looked more sinister than Red Ridinghood's wolf. My body retightened. Then, Monsieur Elal commanded me to "marchez vite," just the way the soldier at the airport had done. My insides jumped back into the jeep.

My body stayed put, though. I picked up my small bag and followed M. Elal who had by then mounted my large (I do mean large) trunk on his head as easily as if it was a five pound sack of potatoes. Trying to keep up with him, see the sites and keep out of the ruts and gullies, I stumbled…often.

What in the world is that smell?

Again the strange, stringent smell had traveled like a shot up my nostrils and flipped my stomach, without one detour. I could not imagine what would produce a smell so strong. But by the time I passed my third trash and garbage heap along the path, I knew. What I did not know was that the smell of rot and waste would be a constant companion during my entire stay. There would be no truck waking me up any morning, grinding its loud gears, dumping and compacting.

Somehow, I will just have to get used to the smell and not allow it to make me sick.

I squeezed my right hand so tightly that nail prints were in my palms for hours. Needed strength and courage just to continue walking.

"You are lucky. You have a house with electricity and a toilet," the VentureFar agents had told me. That "luck" meant little as my new home came into view. I marveled it was still standing.

As far as the toilet is concerned, what I got hardly qualified in my book. I knew I would have to use it, though. Had I tried to use a latrine, squatting over that hole in the ground would have crunched my 58-year old arthritic knees and I probably would have been left in that position…forever.

◄ ► ▼ ▲

My African home was five rooms built side by side in a long row. The three center rooms had an anteroom in front with frames for three picture windows and two entrance doors. Not a pane or door panel was anywhere in sight. The portion of the anteroom in front of my door, served as my dining room. The rest was a playroom where children sometimes played or slept on the floor.

Though years of grime, crack and crumble showed in the house's blocks and cement, the tin roof gleamed. It was no doubt put on in anticipation of my arrival. The shiny, silver roof looked out of place in its newness.

Looking at the house, you knew that no painting or washing had been done…probably since its construction. That included the two-room building that served as the kitchen, too.

Chris would take one look at all this and say, "Ooooo, filthy McNasty."

My host family included the father and his two wives. One wife had two children and the other had none (a terrible thing in Africa). Also, the father's sister lived in the house with her two daughters. I later learned that a nephew had lived there, but now lived with his "femme" and her children on the other side of the village. I got his room.

The moment M. Elal and I reached the yard, the chatter began. Not ever having heard conversational French spoken by villagers, I was initially baffled. Wished I had studied French longer.

Narrowly focusing, I comprehended what was being said, but couldn't respond. My brain simply would not interpret, formulate French responses in rapid succession, then command my lips to speak. It got stuck on visuals, ignoring my need to make sounds.

"I know these people! I know these people! In fact, there is Aunt Lou. Is this where she came after she died? Oh, stop silly! There's Jeff's Aunt Leila!

"Est-ce que vous voulez vous coucher Madame Talbin?"

"Madame Talbin? Madame Talbin! Madame Talbin!"

I am not sure how long I had been standing there suspended (probably with my mouth wide open), but when I finally heard my name, I was able to answer, somewhat. Was mighty grateful my brain had started to shift. M. Elal had taken the trunk into my room and thought maybe I wanted to take a nap before dinner.

"O-u-i M-o-n-s-i-e-u-r. M-e-r-c-i."

My answer must have been one of the longest in the history of the French language. Probably sounded much like when White folks talk in Shetland. My brain had slowed everything down as if it was running out of steam. I think the residual shock from the smell and seeing people who looked exactly like ones I knew had altered normal cooperation between all my senses. Only forced concentration enabled my legs to move and follow M. Elal inside.

My room was small. A single bed stood in its center surrounded by an open mosquito net strung from the ceiling. I could tell the netting was new, it was still white. Covering the walls, Nooooo, stuck in patches on the walls, were bits of beige, flowered wallpaper. Only the center of each bit still adhered to the wall. The ends were either curled or unevenly torn. Spiders had created unique webbings for their palatial "digs."

Above the entrance door to my room, a light bulb was screwed into a jutting socket whose wiring could not only be seen, but easily touched. Wires crept up the wall in intertwining patterns like distended veins up the arms of an engaged weightlifter. The white, red and green were barely visible through layers and layers and layers of dust and grime.

Opposite the door was a window the size of a ship's porthole if portholes were square. The shutter attached to its sash hung poised to keep out unwanted light. Unfortunately for me, when closed, it also kept out any available outside air. I felt as though I had stepped onto the set of an ancient movie. My eyes searched for Boris Korloff. I knew this had to be the very room where Frankenstein slept when he was not in the laboratory.

Wobbling from exasperation and exhaustion, I plopped down on the bed. Before I could think what to do next, Madame Elal #1 was standing in the doorway beckoning for the two buckets sitting in the corner next to my trunk. I gave them to her, closed the door and sat back on the bed to catch my breath and take a stab at regaining my composure.

Josephine, the oldest of M. Elal's girls, knocked on the door a while later.

"Come, come, your water is ready," she said in a heavy French accent.

I so wanted a good hot bath after traveling all that way. Needed to shampoo my hair, too. Can you imagine my feelings when Josephine led me out of the house, across the courtyard, behind a wall, alongside the building used for cooking? With a wide, bright smile, she opened the center door in a bank of three stalls, and with palms up, extended her arms in a "go inside" gesture. As soon as I was in, she quickly handed me a key and closed the door. There I was again, standing with my mouth opened, wondering.

The two buckets Mme Elal had taken sat filled with water on the floor just in front of a seatless commode. The water was slightly brown. A large plastic cup floated in the bucket on the left. I stood there looking, but not understanding or really believing what I saw. Slowly, ever so slowly, the realization that no hot bath or shampoo would happen that day seeped into my consciousness. Though I had attended every cross-cultural session VentureFar provided, none of what I heard seemed real until that very moment.

Ooooooooookay, Robin ol' girl. You wanted to come home to Africa. You've got it! Here you are! Now what?

Despite my shock, or maybe because of it, I started using my old reliable problem-solving technique: Assess, reason, then decide.

Canata has her hisses, I have the decision-making technique that always works for me. Do your thing, technique!

I saw there was no tank on the commode to hold water for flushing. So I knew I would probably have to use one of the buckets of water for that. There was no tissue, so I needed to go back into my room and get one of the rolls I had been advised to bring.

"Thank goodness for VentuFar training!"

There was a square indentation in the floor with what looked like a draining hole in its left corner.

So, that is obviously where I should...shower? Oh, that's what that cup is for!

Passersby could see my bag of toiletries, wash puff, towel and pink silk pajamas lying across the ledge of the stall's window cutout (no pane there either). I could see them staring as they walked by. They probably thought my things an odd collection and wondered, *Whatever do you do with that round puffy ball thing?*

You want to know why I took silk pajamas? Well since childhood, the feel of silk on my skin has abated my anxieties. Thought my pajamas might be useful at the end of an especially troublesome day. Didn't know how badly I would need them day one. Was happy I had brought my other familiar things, too.

Slowly I lathered, dipped and poured until I felt reasonably refreshed. Then, returned to my room and cut a deal with the spiders.

"If you don't bother me, I won't bother you! Understand?"

I found a comfortable sink in my mattress, tightly tucked the netting underneath and stretched out with a long audible sigh. Before I completely exhaled…. "Knock, knock, knock!" Dinner had been served. I didn't want to get out of bed even to eat, but I was hungry.

To skip dinner my first night would be rude!

I dragged myself up and went to the table in the anteroom. There, I sat and waited, and waited and waited for the family to join me. No one was in sight, not even the children who since my arrival had constantly filled the yard gabbing in their village tongue and staring at me as if I was an animal in a stall at the zoo. There was just me, the food and a big margouillat that scooted up the wall intermittently pausing to bob up and down and stare. I could hear his lizard comrades darting across the roof, making raindrop sounds that reminded me of Shetland. Cousin Sissy and I had spent many days and nights listening to the sounds of raindrops falling on Auntee Vee's tin roof. We even made up scary stories to match their patterns. The scariest story would be the one for the slow drips at the end of a rainshower.

Remembering my cross-cultural training, I realized no one would join me. I would eat alone until I extended an invitation. Even then, because I was older, only the father would (or could) accept. That night, I chose to eat alone. Didn't see anyone to invite anyway.

Ooooooo, rice!

I was delightfully surprised when I lifted the covers from the bowls. I recognized what was in three of them. Being my adventurous self, I spooned what I thought was redeye gravy over my rice, not knowing that fifteen minutes later, I would have tiny welts on my body and big, fat lips. Before I heaped a fish onto my plate though, I had to behead it. Quickly re-covered that bowl so those eyes wouldn't stare at me while I ate the body. The taste was a little foreign, but palatable.

"Thank you VentuFar for furnishing and teaching me how to use my medical kit." Now where's that Benadryl injector?

While retucking my netting, I heard dishes clinking. Someone was clearing the table. Only then did I remember the delicious pineapple slices I had left behind. I wanted them badly, but there was no way I was getting out of my bed, again.

Who is that, I wondered. *Where were they when I was eating? This is getting too weird. Come on sleep! Maybe things will look different tomorrow.*

The next morning, I was awakened by "Swish, swish, swiiiissh; swish, swish, swiiiisssh."

"What? What in the world...?"

I listened intently for a while, but could not identify the sound. Got up and cracked the door for a look. Saw Josephine bent over sweeping the courtyard with something that looked like a bunch of thin sticks tied together at one end, then spread out in broomlike fashion.

I learned that every morning it was Josephine's duty to sweep the entire compound, bring two gigantic buckets of water from the village pump (about a half-mile away), wash dishes and scrub pots and pans before walking the three miles to school. Though only 14, she was a young village woman in training and the mark of a "proper" village woman is that her courtyard is cleanly swept, dishes washed and pots and pans shiny at the beginning of each day.

Thinking all of this too much for a young school girl to do, I got up early one morning and offered help. The gesture made Josephine so uncomfortable that she avoided me for days. I knew better, but sometimes my old "fix it" and "save the world" selves can not be contained, cross-cultural training or no.

▼ ◄ ► ▲

It didn't take long before I knew that the racism and religious ostracism challenges I had wrestled with in the past that kept my eyes peeled toward Africa, had been replaced by "genderism." In Africa, the word "woman" was synonymous with drudgery and servitude. Sometimes I painfully watched women for over 18 hours, fulfill servitous, sacrificial tasks just to eke out meager rationings for the following day. Forget the gender scales being balanced, those women had no idea the scales even existed.

I cried openly, seeing the plight of village women. It seemed they were only considered human when a service of some kind was needed. What bothered me even more was that they seemed resigned to their condition as though it was fated and there was nothing they could do to change it.

A village woman's daily routine began at daybreak. After the yard was swept, she chopped wood for a fire before walking to the market. Returning home, she built the fire, cooked and served breakfast and got her children off to school. Those things done, she went to the fields to do her days work or off to the market to sell what she spent most of the night preparing.

At day's end, I often saw Mme. Elal#1 coming down the road from the fields balancing on her head a big (I mean real BIG) pan of manioc, giant potato-looking roots five times the size of any sweet potato I ever saw and I belonged to 4H. In the evenings, even after working in the fields all day long, she had to performed the wood collecting, fire building, cooking and serving routine again. This time, she also had to pound "foutou" that like bread, was served with sauce at every meal.

Foutou looks and tastes like…"ugh." To make it, either manioc, bananas, or ignames (more like white potatoes) were pounded into a stiff mush and served in batches that looked much like the dough Granny used to place on the sideboard to rise before baking her much sought-after rolls.

Because foutou needed pounding every day (seven days a week), families had there own wooden mortar and pestle set used only to prepare it. That is, unless someone in the family was a traditional healer. Then, the set might be used to pulverize and ready roots and herbs for distribution to those seeking a potion.

Weekdays, Mme Elal#1 had no one to help her with any of the chores. Mme Elal#2 was away with M. Elal in the fields for the week, M. Elal's sister was at the market selling whatever she had prepared the night before and the children would not get home from school until late. She worked harder than I had ever seen Granny work.

Want to hear the story of the biggest lie I ever told? You know about my stories! But, I promise this will be the very last one. Listen:

I visited a family in a neighboring village with a friend. The family was real happy to see Oneka and to meet her visitor who had come all the way from "l'Amerique." The wife, Guila, was preparing something special. She asked if I wanted foutou or rice with my meal. "Rice," I replied, since I couldn't stand the dough consistency of foutou.

Oneka and I sat in the circle of men, as was the custom for older, visiting women. The men were all drinking "Bangui." I couldn't join them. Never acquired a taste for palm wine. It tasted like extra strong vinegar to me. Everybody was laughing and catching up on "les nouvelles." I was just trying to understand what news they were sharing as best I could and wishing again I had studied French longer.

When dinner was served, I heaped my plate with rice and reached for the sauce. But when I removed the saucepot lid, I stared at some strange looking...feet. Not to appear awkward, I scooped out a little sauce (avoiding the feet) and passed the pot along. The host took one look at my plate and began questioning.

"Why didn't you take the meat? It is for you, it is for you," he insisted in French I readily understood. Naughty me, with my quick thinking self, I told the biggest, fattest lie ever. And it just rolled off my tongue as if it was the beautiful truth.

"I am a vegetarian. I don't eat meat. Soooo, someone else can have it, if they want. Why don't you take it? Something special for the man of the family."

That day, I convinced them I was not simply vegetarian, but "vegan." No meat or animal by-products ever! Hoped they were impressed that I took a little of the sauce.

Guess what? Later, I found out that the foot was from an agouti (bush rat), a staple for villagers. But not for me.

"It's good! It tastes like a cross between chicken and lamb," people told me. But that made it worse. *"No mongrel flesh for me, thank you!"* Besides, there were too many other African dishes I had tasted and loved.

"Poissons et ignames frites avec du piment, c'est magnifique!"

Each time I ate that combination it reminded me of the hot fried fish sandwich and French fries I always bought when the church back in Shetland had its Friday night fundraisers. Just thinking about a piece of that golden brown mullet being lifted dripping from the hot grease in the black wash pot made my mouth water. I could just see it all golden brown on the long handle fork willed by Miss Lizzie's able hands. When the fish landed between the two pieces of "light bread" layed out on wax paper, the next sounds were the sizzle made by hotsauce and mustard meeting the heat and my hearty "Ummmmmmmm umm."

While African women in villages did the ten-zillion chores in their survival routine, the men usually sat watching. I got the impression they felt entitled to sit and rest at the end of their day in the fields.

None of that "woman's work" for them!

How familiar is that?

One day I thoughtfully studied a man pruning a backyard tree. Thought about my old chinaberry tree and hoped its limbs were still in tact. Wondered if anyone sat in its limbs the way I did as a child.

When the man finished chopping, every leaf and limb was left laying in wait for women who came with their strong hands wrapped tightly around sharpened machetes. The man sat and watched the chopping, lifting, toting and sweeping until the yard was again clean.

Every once in a while when I walked through the village, I saw one or two men weaving fishing baskets…while they sat. Never saw them hauling even one batch of fish they had caught.

Maintaining the survival routine seemed burdensome for every woman I saw. It was no lighter for those with small children or even pregnant women. On any given day, I saw pregnant women along the roadside returning home from the fields with the same big pans of manioc on their heads as other women. Sometimes, she had a small baby on her back and two or three little ones walking alongside. The small children needed to be protected from being sucked in by the backdraft of speeding cars and trucks. Every time I saw this, I got angry. Had no idea toward whom my anger should be directed.

I really need lots of help to understand this:

Do I get mad at the girl? Chances are she is a victim. Do I vent my anger toward the culture that perpetuates these customs? They could simply be holding on to the sense of order that keeps them sane. Am I responsible in any way? If so, what can I really do to help when there are so many and I am only one?

I had a variation of this conversation with myself and anyone who would listen many, many times before I left Alemokon. Each time ended in more and more questions and fewer and fewer answers.

Young village women were often used like Marvin's "ho's," but without pay. Rape was so prevalent that it enjoyed a hushed accommodation. Only the girl suffered when the act was made public. She would be isolated and not even allowed to practice her religious traditions with others. She was the community "bad girl." I remember when one young girl was publicly flogged after giving birth to the rape-child. The man's name? Not one whisper, though everyone knew who he was, knew he was much older and knew he had forced her into submission.

Ummmmmmmph," I often screamed inside, squeezing both my hands with my eyes tightly shut. But the only response I got was mounting frustration and deepening anger.

I don't know how long I can withstand this! While everybody treats me good, what about my sisters?

Will there ever be a place where women can just...Be? A place where we can freely and fully express without having to limit ourselves, simply because we're women? Must we always be burdened by the dictates of others? Who should define who we are and what we should do, anyway?

"Ummmmmmmmmmmmmmmmmmmmph."

Ooooookay, Robin ol' girl. Settle down. Don't let these conditions push you into running away. You know you need to stay at least the four months left on your contract. You have to see this through! Do what you can to help. Just stand for a while and calm yourself down.

▲ ▶ ▼ ◀

"While I am calming Dear Reader, let me tell you about the village of Alemokon. Perhaps you will want to see it for yourself one day."

Alemokon, is divided into four "Quartiers." Each has its own chief.

Most of the educated villagers with what is considered "proper" incomes live in the Quartier Paris. *(This is almost the same as where Black folk live in Shetland. Interesting.)* Those living in Paris are either Government workers themselves, or relatives of someone in a Governmental position.

Paris's big houses sit high on the hill and are easily seen from the roads below. The architecture of one or two of the houses would rival any in America, if they were constructed from brick instead of cinderblock. Every time I walked pass one of those houses, sentiments of "home" filled my head and heart. However, when I finally got on the inside, all my sentiment melted.

The inside walls were unpainted. Furnishings were too dark, too ornate, overstuffed and worn. Pictures hung on walls seemingly with no thought having been given to size, shape or content. I never figured out why, but they always hung slightly lopsided. Every crease, crack and crevice was filled with red and gray dust. I knew they could not help the dust, but it was still a nightmare for the tidy housekeeper I think myself to be. Inside of the homes was for me, depressing, but interesting.

A major drawback to living in Paris was getting up and down the hill. During the short rainy season while I was there, driving up in red clay without getting stuck and sliding backwards was a miracle. When it was dry, the trip was dusty and sometimes sprinkled with bandits waiting to like Robinhood, "take from the rich...." Well, maybe not like Robinhood, since I doubt if any of the booty was ever given to anyone else.

The rest of the villagers live in the other three Quartiers. Three or four houses, shacks and huts were grouped around a common yard. These clusters are a stunning contrast to the single houses on the hill with their big individual yards often walled for privacy. Most homes in the three Quartiers are without electricity or running water. The few that have, most likely belong to the chief, one of his siblings or children. One house with electricity is always the designated keeper of the Quartier's radio and TV, primarily used to receive and desiminate local and world news to interested villagers.

Having struggled on little money while rearing my children, I thought I knew hardship. "But, noooooo!" The conditions in Alemokon showed me that I had never even seen hardship. Neither had I ever really imagined it. Couldn't. Hardship is what shows in the hands and on the feet of even young village women, those in their early 20s, after years of performing their survival routine. Such leathery, crusty skin I had never before seen on women.

I also thought I had seen poverty. "But, nooooooo!" The ghettos I had seen in America would be "high living" for some of the villagers.

Visiting in the Quartiers did not mean a knock on the door and a "Hello, come in." Generally, when I walked into a courtyard, I had to first engage in a greeting ritual that included asking for and reporting the news the way the men did when Oneka and I visited the village and I told the big lie. Only then, could I state my particular business. If I came to see someone, I had to sit outside and wait until the person was found. Or, wait until the contact dismissed me by granting me "the road" I knew was customary to ask for before leaving.

Never could I wait in the courtyard alone, or sit any place else alone for that matter. Privacy seemed not to be a concept villagers understood. They would go out of their way to make sure I always had company. If they saw me sitting by myself, they asked "why," then stopped whatever they were doing or wherever they were going to stay with me until someone else came. I knew if I wanted to just sit and think I could not do it outside where anyone was likely to see. Having lived alone for many years, it took a while for me to feel totally comfortable with that level of concern.

Walking around in the village, I had to always dodge "les moutons et poulets" freely roaming. If I wasn't very careful, "plat, plat" right into the middle of the droppings left by these goats and chickens. The rainy season was the worse. I not only had to watch out for squishy droppings, but try and keep from slipping into red-mud ruts at the same time. Did I ever? Only once and that was one time too many.

Getting from village to village is <u>real</u> interesting. If I wanted to go to another village, I walked up to the main road and waited for a "voiture" onto which I could climb. I probably should have said, "into which...," since transport was usually an old pick-up truck with a tarp-covered back sagging from dropping into too many ruts with too many bodies, boxes and bags stuffed inside. I could hear the truck coming from miles away. I am sure that the mechanisms in its motor had long since forgotten the feel and taste of premium oil. Had probably forgotten the color and smell, too. Could you "climb in" or "hang on" was all that mattered to the voiture driver and his mechanic who also doubled as faretaker.

What is a schedule? Oh, I remember. That is one of those time things for buses, trains, and planes in America. Hummmmmmm.

Everybody I met in Alemokon wanted to live in America. To hear them talk, you would think America was heaven.

"Here is my address and a telephone number where you can reach me. Will you take me back to America with you?"

"When you leave, can I go with you?

I hated the questions. Would have loved to say "Yes" to each one But since I knew I could only answer in the negative, each time I was asked, I interpreted the question as an expression of hopelessness. Knew that instead of giving the escape sought, I would soon leave all askers with one more nail of rejection driven into their proverbial coffin.

While I am getting into my car driving to a fine restaurant for Italian cuisine, they will be hard at work from dawn to late-night just to put food in their bowls. Feeling thirsty, glass in hand, I will walk to my water dispenser and fill it not only with clean water that's safe to drink, but cooled to my liking. They on the other hand, will still tote big buckets of dingy water filled with all sorts of infectious contaminants that they can only hope are not lethal. Instead of calling a construction company, they will still make home repairs by throwing clumps of mud into the empty holes washed away by the rain. Or, repair the roof by laying new branches and leaves at just the right angles to disallow seepage. Some will unroll large sheets of green plastic, cover their homes and hold it down with whatever large boulders they can find.

Ummmmmmmmph! Here I go again. But, who is to blame for how people live? The Government? God? If the Alemokon lifestyle is either of their will, what can be done? What can I do?

I would tell you a story about the time a delegation of men came to try and talk me into taking M. Elal home with me, but I promised you had heard the last story. Remember? I can say this though: I never figured out what they thought M. Elal could do that would be so "very, very helpful" to me. I never saw him go to the fields, do any work around the house and he certainly was no artisan.

Excuse me while I play a game of Solitaire. Maybe that will help me calm a bit more and change my thinking. No matter what I say about Alemokon, it is a place you will need to see for yourself to fully appreciate.

On my way to catch a voiture one day, a wonderful thing happened. A blue and red soccer ball bounced, then rolled into my path, halting me in mid-step. The ball stopped right at the point where my foot would have landed. Thank goodness, I looked down in time to hop over it without falling. Just as I looked up, I heard, "pardon taunte" and saw the face of a most handsome young man. He was even more gorgeous than Bobby, the Italian boy who sat in front of me in high school.

What beautiful grandchildren he and Ellie could give me, I thought. Then, I wondered if she was really serious about that Pierre boy she wrote about in her letters.

Diallo was already six feet tall and only 12. In French, his mandated language, "Noir" means black, but does not account for the glistening, deep-brown overcast that glowed from Diallo's skin. His eyes beamed like two full moons in a midnight sky. His voice and smile somehow lit up my mind and began changing the tenor of my thoughts. For the first time, I saw beauty in Alemokon. Probably because Diallo reminded me of Sam and whenever I thought of Sam those days, I always felt warmth and wonderment.

Where would I be had I married Sam instead of Jeff? Would I be first wife? Or even, queen? Next week when I am in the big village, I'll need to make arrangements for my trip to visit him.

Madame Roble, a cousin to Mme Elal#2 came into view carrying a sack of …I don't know what, comfortably balanced atop her head. I saw not how burdened down she was, but how erect and gracefully she walked.

Diallo had simply picked up and threw the ball to his eagerly awaiting comrades. I am sure he never knew the difference he had made.

I stood for a moment and watched the young men maneuver and kick the ball. It was interesting to see what tactics they used to advance the ball and not touch it with their hands. Nobody wanted the ball to be turned over to the opposing team. Once play began, those tall, willowy young men moved like a whole herd of cheetahs spooked by a sudden threat. They were so intense in their play that butting heads, trips and falls drew little attention. Whatever happened, they simply set up the next play.

The boys started to pay attention to my standing there. So, I broke my gaze and moved on.

I decided to walk the three kilometers to the next village. Wanted to look at things through my "new" eyes. Also, to see if there were other things of beauty I had been missing. My knees needed the exercise, anyway.

I actually looked into the faces of everybody I met that afternoon. Initiated greetings, too. Every person got a hearty "bonjour." Some of the grownups responded, some did not. But, every child gave me a smile and a "bonjour tante" or "bonjour mamma," depending on their age and how old they thought I was.

Down the road I noticed what looked like a big beautiful bouquet. It wasn't a bouquet of flowers, but a group of women colorfully dressed to go...I didn't know where. But I did know it must have been important. Otherwise, they would not have interrupted their survival routine.

Later I learned they were on their way to support a mother who was burying her two-year old daughter found floating in the marigot two days before.

A few times a year, a young child's lifeless body was pulled from the marigot. Nothing was ever done to close off the stream like one would think. Because for many villagers, the water was central to their survival, it couldn't be fenced. Besides, where would they find that much fencing and who would pay for it? Had the villagers devoted their resources to such project, the expense and subsequent limited access would probably have caused many more deaths than what the marigot took. Every bit that every member of the family earned was desperately needed to support living.

Whenever a child died, everyone took time away from their routine to support the family. They shared each other's grief, knowing it could be their child, grandchild, or other loved one next.

The women formed a lovely bouquet in their colorful wrappings and drapings. Their uncovered faces displayed like the center of a very large bloom. As I got closer, the patterns in the cloth could be distinguished. There were circles, squares, splotches and swirls. Some prints were of animals, masks and other ritualistic icons. One pattern made me think about the material Granny had bought me with its large blooms and brown splotches on a royal blue background. I felt a tinge of the hurt I had felt when the acid dropped on my dress that day at the science fair.

That was so long ago. Why do I still feel that?

It doesn't make sense, but I still feel it.

Some of the cloth had cameos of White religious figures and politicians who had sometimes proven corrupt. These made me wonder, "Why?" But even their pictures were surrounded by rich, bright color.

The women were a sea of beauty in an otherwise drab scene. I had often wondered what could possibly give joy to people living in the conditions I found in Alemokon. Back home, such conditions would have garnered pity or scorn.

Suddenly, my mind's light illuminated with a loud "click."

Now it all makes sense that Black people love loud colors, loud music and flashy cars. Loudness and flash lifts spirits. For a time, they can enjoy stimulating imagery that helps to blot out their sufferings. Loud music... joy! Loud colors and fast cars... power! Altogether...wonderful life!

I couldn't wait to share this new insight in my letters to Ellie and Chris.

▼ ◄ ► ▲

While writing my nightly letters to my children, I heard loud drumming. I knew that drums were key instruments used for ancient African communication, but I had not heard them until that one night. The sounds rattled my nerves.

Wonder what the drumbeats mean? What message they're sending? Are they sending a warning? Wish I was fluent in "drumese. Do I know anybody who is?"

My wonderings were interrupted by a knock. It was Josephine, asking if I had planned to attend the church "fete." I made plans.

I got up early that Sunday morning. Wanted to make sure I was dressed on time and had packed enough film to cover everything.

"The priest only comes once every three months or so," Josephine told me. "We must have all the christenings, ordinations and marriages when he comes."

I also dressed early, because I wanted to give my clothes time to lose more wrinkles. Only the tailor had an iron in the village and it was too late to have him press anything when Josephine reminded me about the festival.

Leaving out of my room, I all but crashed into Mme Elal#1. She looked at me with a disgusted frown, then handed me what at first I thought were just pieces of cloth. I was not asked, but told to change. Instead of leaving, she sat and stared as though I needed guarding so I wouldn't bolt. Anger seized my body and mind. I had to fight the urge to say, "No! This is what I'm wearing!" After all, I had on my best linen suit.

Who does she think she is to tell me what to wear, I thought. *How does she have the nerve to frown at my expensive suit and she still lives in Alemokon?*

As soon as the name of the village crossed my mind, I was brought back to my senses.

Alemokon is _her_ *village. She can look any way and do whatever she wants. I am in* _her_ *home. She does not have to value my expensive linen. Her cloth is what's worthwhile here. I need to understand that value or worth is environment specific and be thankful that she wants me to dress like a member of her family. Hummmm, they are my African family, aren't they?*

With that, my urge ebbed and I slowly began changing my clothes. Boy was I glad Mme Elal had stayed.

Traditional village dress for women in Alemokon, Africa, included separate pieces of cloth to be worn for a headwrap, blouse, skirt and an extra piece that wraped around the hips, then tied into a looped, draping off to the left. Wrapping each piece demands a technique and skill I had never used before, in fact, did not have. All African garb I owned, had always been ready to wear.

I don't know how to wrap this so it will stay. Each time I follow the steps in the directions the VentuFar agent gave me, the second I move, it all begin to unravel. The head and skirt wrap alone would probably take me until well after the "fete" is over.

I asked for and got plenty of help. When I was re-dressed, I got a big smile of approval. I even felt I was "looking good." I showed Mme Elal how to operate my camera and was not disappointed with the results.

By the time we arrived, the little church was packed from front to back. People were spilling out of both doors. We were escorted inside where I heard pronouncements by the priest in French, then his words were immediately translated into a local language I didn't understand. When babies were brought to the altar, my camera flashed. When dancers and gifters came down the isle…flash! Most of my film though, was dedicated to the marriages.

I hope all of my pictures are clear. I want to share every bit of this day with Ellie, Chris and Hanan.

I don't know about you, but when I think of a wedding, I envision a young giddy couple who just know their love will conquer all, though so many others' have failed. But in Alemokon, both couples were well past their 50s. They had taken their civil and cultural vows when they were young and had few possessions. Had reared their children and one couple was rearing their grands. Only now, could they afford the luxury of a ceremony "religieuse."

I admired those couples the same way I had revered couples back home who renewed their marriage vows in formal ceremonies. They seemed to be shouting to the world, "Our love has conquered all" and promising to rely on the strength of their love "until death." For me, a hopeless romantic, that is a worthwhile goal toward which we all should strive.

The marriages were also the focus of the villagers' attention. After the ceremonies ended, everyone filled the streets with dancing and singing to tunes played by a six-piece brass and drum band, a la New Orleans. The crowd swayed side to side in time with the pulsating rhythms. With arched backs, hops and shuffles villagers expressed their joy in dance.

Oh, that is what the drumming was for! They were practicing! Wanted to make sure every beat was right. I see the trumpeters are older, so maybe they didn't need to practice.

The horns blew loudly and the drummers drummed hard. No ear could escape the merriment. Even the misting rain did not dampen the revelers' spirits and magnanimous enthusiasm with which they surrounded the couples. Each couple was gleefully escorted to their separate courtyards where the wedding feast was prepared and waiting.

Flash! Flash! Flash!

Our family went to each courtyard. We ate, drank and shared repeated embraces. By the day's end, I felt I had finally been swallowed in the Black love and warmth I sought. Truly felt I was where I should be. That night, I enjoyed the most peaceful rest I had had since my arrival.

▼ ◄ ► ▲

In the morning, I went immediately to the anteroom table to begin sharing my joyful experiences. Midway through my second letter, it happened.

Blam! Blam! Blop! Bloop! Doors and shutters were slamming. In a flurry, first one way and then another, mothers gathered children snatching them by their arms, clothes or anything else they could grab to drag them inside.

I was sitting at the table, pen suspended in mid air looking around like a ventriloquist's dummy. My head was turning side-to-side and eyes rolling trying to take in all the confusion at once.

Josephine, running but saying nothing, grabbed my arm, jerked me into my room and slammed shut both my door and shutters. She kneeled next to my bed and began to pray. I don't know why, but I kneeled too. Whatever was happening, I didn't think prayer could hurt.

Shortly, I heard the pops of gunshots and roaring motors. Heard the loud panting sounds and running footsteps of both the pursuers and pursued. Josephine prayed louder. She kept me inside for what seemed like hours after the last sounds faded into the distance.

The sun was never brighter and air never fresher than when we emerged from my room that day. People mattered, not surroundings or things. Life became dearer and dearer the more Josephine recounted stories of other times the rebels had come to Alemokon. Happily this time, they only passed through.

Many Countries in Africa were enduring revolutionary change. They were moving from the old "rule by birthright" system toward a new democracy. Struggles between the old and new guards were plentiful. Sometimes, they erupted into military battles that spilled over into villages that like Alemokon, were near the Capitol city. In one year, Alemokon had been caught up in two successful "coup d'etats" and two attempts. Military responses to public demonstrations in the Capitol had left over two hundred bodies lying lifeless in the streets in one day. Mass graves were unearthed bearing bodies of young men, their mysteries yet unsolved. I felt as if I had stepped so far back in time that I should do something to save my five-room "Tara," even without the help of Clark Gable.

The keeper of the Quartier's radio blasted news from morning to night for the next few days. The rebels failed to seize the main radio station. Six were killed in the attempt. All the gory details of their deaths were broadcasted for all to hear. The President's "things are under control" speech was played over and over and over and ....

Okay! We get the point! We hear that you are in charge and the rebels have been beaten back, again! Enough already!

Quickly, things got back to normal in the village, except for the constant blare of the radio. Villagers were going about their usual survival routines. I seemed to be the only one still upset. Had never before considered that this journey could result in my death. That disturbed me to the core.

While writing my letters, I felt I was writing to people in some land far, far away with which I had little or no connection. Had to constantly remind myself that these were letters to relatives and friends. Letters to my children.

After a mere four and a half months, Africa possessed me. She had demanded a commitment far beyond what anything or anybody else had ever done, even my children and students. I had responded with helpless surrender.

Has Africa brainwashed me with Her heat, living conditions and constant military threats? Is that what has ripped away my confidence? I feel like a mush ball. For some reason, I feel I need to stay here for the life of the contract. But...why? I can easily go home right now.

One thing is certain: You can not be emotionally tentative and remain in an African village. You need to stay strong, alert and focused if you want to survive.

In Alemokon, I felt my life always at risk. It was as if Mother Africa had turned on me and was now my enemy.

If the heat doesn't get me, the spiders and mosquitoes probably will with their deadly stings. If malaria doesn't get me, the other germs carried by the children, dogs, chickens or goats might. If the bandits don't get me, there are the soldiers with their surprise attacks. If the food doesn't get....

Stop it, Robin! Remember beauty? Look at the beautiful sky!

Just think. That is the same sky under which Cousin Sissy and I used to sit in the yard and make up names for cloud shapes when we were in Shetland. Amazing.

Wow! Have those palm trees always been there?

For the first time I noticed that some of the palms were shaped like Spanish fans swaying back and forth, offering coolness from the hot African sun. There were palms shaped like fountains spewing water up from the center of a pond. Their dark, layered, bulbous roots completed the illusion. The elephant-eared palm with which I was most familiar, grew liberally all around. They all served as a wonderful backdrop for lots and lots of colorful blooms. Many of the blooms hung in clusters as though Mother Nature herself was handing me a special bouquet.

As I sat observing the scenery, a male lizard tried to run from one side of the anteroom to the other. Had it been the less colorful female, my "shoo" and flailing arms would have run her off. But the male with his beautifully blended shades of orange and gray and his African male nature, stopped, bobbed his body up and down and stared right into my eyes as if saying, "I am going this way and little woman, you can't stop me no matter what! You better move!"

"Ha! One thing you forgot Mr. Margouillat bud, I am bigger than you are. Soooooo, if anybody changes his course here, it will be you! Now, shoo!"

Oh sh-t! I am going mad! I'm sitting here talking to a d—n lizard. Folks back home would really get a kick out of this. Some thought it; some said it and now it's really true. I AM LOOOOONEY TUNES!

It was then that I acknowledged the cramping pains in my stomach. I had had cramps for days. Dismissed them. Gas. The pains were harder than ever, but I figured if I just sat still and relaxed for a while, the cramps would stop. They didn't. That night, Africa claimed not only my emotions and my psyche, but also my insides. By the next evening, trips I had made back and forth across the courtyard to the toilet, declined into rollovers onto my sides while Josephine and Mme Elal changed and washed my sheets. I felt as if I had been tossed into the "ol' lake of fire" Granny used to threaten me with when I was little. Everything I ate or drank was immediately reclaimed. After two days, I didn't even have the strength to roll. I felt as though I was dying. Breathing was becoming harder and harder.

I can't die here. Too far from home. What about Ellie and Chris? I have got to see my first grandchild that's due any day now.

My next convulsion left me too weak to fight. I would just have to accept the inevitable. So I relaxed my right hand and drifted off.

What I thought was the "grim reaper" handing me over to the angels, turned out to be the VentuFar agent carrying me to his jeep to take me to a hospital in the Capitol. I remember nothing of the trip and only snipits of the next I don't know how many days. My first real recollection was feeling the coolness of sheets and someone gently rubbing my arm while calling my name. I opened my eyes to see a smiling black face vignetted in a sea of whiteness. Just knew it was an angel welcoming me to my "mighty kingdom." But it was a nurse.

"Madame Talbin! Madame Talbin! Ca va? Ca va, Madame Talbin? Ca va mieux?"

I didn't feel strong enough to speak, so I just nodded to let her know I had heard. I knew she understood that since I consciously responded, I must have felt better.

Feeling life flow back into my body, I decided I would not give up. I would fight Mother Africa for my life. I would have the last say in how and where I died. It would not be so far away from my children. Chris would never forgive me for not welcoming his first born. I used every bit of my gradually returning strength to escalate my fight.

By the time I was able to leave the hospital, a little more than one month was left on my contract. I decided mostly on the advice of my doctor, not to return to Alemokon. VentureFar found me a small apartment near the hospital so I could continue my treatments. They even hired an attendant.

How will I say goodbye to people in Alemokon? Maybe I will go in the jeep with the driver when he goes to pick up my things.

But the doctor said I shouldn't go back. That I would risk re-infection.

I'll figure it out later. There is no way I can leave and not let them know how grateful I am for all they have done for me, epecially my family. They took time from their survival routine to make their way to the hospital to visit me. I want them to know that I will always love and miss them. Afterall, we have been through a lot together during this short time.

◀▼▶▲

Moving into the apartment, I was happy I didn't have to live there but a month. The whole complex was encased in high walls with a big solid steel gate for access and 24-hour guards. I felt imprisoned. Trapped.

Where is everybody? This is an eery quiet. Scary. Ten times worse than living in the projects. At least there, people came outside and mingled. The only people I have seen are guards.

What I saw on my first day's walk to the hospital escalated my concern. High walls and solid steel gates surrounded each of the houses and apartment buildings along the route. At many of the entrances, a shed was built right into the wall to house the guardian, similar to construction I had seen in some of the gated communities where many of my friends lived. Only back home, the wall surrounded the entire community, not each house.

Why would people want to live encased in walls? How can they stand being closed off like that? Am I missing something here? Is there some certain danger I should consider?

Trying to understand, I asked and asked and asked. I asked so many questions that I was afraid people would think me a detective…or spy. In a way, I guess I was. I <u>was</u> investigating. Trying to track down a logical explanation for the walling phenomenon. The main difference was that I didn't work for any agency.

But how would anybody know that?

One of the things "sleuth Robin" noted was that in a single block, there might be big mansions with little shantytowns between them. In fact, the first site I saw when walking out of my gate was a shantytown with four one-room lean-tos. Out of the lean-to closest to my gate, I saw a mother and I never got an accurate count of how many children, entering and exiting every day.

The shantytowns were not walled. The families were poor. Uneducated transplants from villages that in most cases, still held on to their village ways. Their very young children walked around naked except for a string of beads around their necks and/or around their waists much of the time. They simply needed a place to live; were happy to have a home. Did not feel it needed to be guarded. Who would want to take it?

The mothers in the shantytowns performed survival routines similar to those I had seen performed by mothers in villages. A major difference was that since there were no fields in which they could work during the day, the city mothers sold whatever they could from a makeshift covered vending table strategically placed at the edge of their courtyards. Early in the morning, you could smell the fish, ignames and planktons frying. I left before determining on what day they sold which items. I bought bananas and roasted peanuts whenever they were displayed.

Seeing the conditions in the shantytowns, I often struggled with my "save the world" self. My greatest struggle came when I went to the dumpster.

As soon as the shantytown children saw me exit the gate with trash bags to put into the "poubelle," they ran and all but snatched them from my hands. They ravaged the bags pulling out any bottles, cans and plastic boxes. No container ever made it to the dumpster. I didn't take time to try and figure out why they wanted them, just started putting containers into a separate bag. I also included papers and magazines, thinking the children might enjoy looking at the pictures. Don't know if they ever got to see a single picture, since on my way back to the apartment, I would see familiar pages wrapped around palm leaves filled with the hot foods the mothers sold.

Do those who live in the mansions struggle with guilt like I do? Could that be one of the reasons they need walls? As they roll up to their "mansions-o-plenty," seated in their luxury cars, perhaps the walls shorten the time they must acknowledge the poor women and children who can barely eat while they feast on imported steaks?

Huummmmmmmmmm.

I don't know what the men who lived in shantytowns did everyday. Only now and then would I see a man go into or come out of a lean-to. Mostly, I saw them at the kiosk drinking café latte. The moment I entered a kiosk, they started smiling. I could tell when one of them had gotten the word and was about to make his pitch.

Men in the City were as aggressive in their "wooings" as men had been in Alemokon. Everywhere I went, a grinning man offered lighthearted chatter, his address and a way to reach him by telephone. What they didn't know was that I already knew why. I knew they too wanted to live in America. News traveled fast by word of mouth in Africa, so I knew they had gotten word of the American women living in the apartment on the corner. I knew they saw me, not as a prospect for romance, but a sponsor. Since I was older, they probably thought I could well afford sponsorship.

A difference between the wooers in the village and those in the city was age. City wooers were considerably younger. Generally when I told them I would be leaving in less time than it took to finalize their travel arrangements, they disappeared. One didn't. He came almost daily to share the intriguing similarities of our life experiences. When we talked, at no time did we have cause for yawn.

▶ ▼ ◀ ▲

I met Dramane in the doctor's waiting room. He was obviously educated and from our conversations, had been a teacher for a number of years before coming to work in the Procurement office for the Ministry of Education. He had been reared in a small village. His parents were Moslems and other close family members Animists, their indigenous religious practice. Though many in Dramane's family had converted to Christianity, none had completely abandoned their old-world beliefs and practices. An uncle had taken Dramane from his village when he was only five to attend school in the city. That was before he was indoctrinated by or initiated into the secret Society that generally shaped the thoughts and practices of young men in the village. Dramane's beliefs were his own.

More than anyone I had ever known, Dramane caused me to take a hard look at my long-held beliefs. Often, our discussions ran well into the night. I shared my life in Shetland, he described what he remembered of life in his village. He shared what he felt were childhood violations, I shared Uncle Ray. For the first time since Group, I had conversations in which I could uncompromisingly bear my soul.

It was our discussions about religion though that raged hot and heavy. I believed Jesus was the only way. Dramane believed no <u>man</u> is. I believed God granted power. He believed power was embedded in humans at birth and was there just waiting to be seized. I believed that all humans are one in spirit. He believed each person to be "a separate entity who works through life as best he can until he rejoins the One Spirit at death."

One night in our discussion though, after sharing my experiences with the saints and telling Dramane how they had crushed my beliefs in the holiness of religion and church, he said some things I found very hard to dispute.

"Dramane, what do you mean by 'holy is what religion is?' All religions are not holy!"

"Dr. Talbin, all religions that honor and serve God are 'holy.' They all espouse spiritual principles and sacred laws that believers can use to conduct supportive, productive, loving and peaceful lives. Isn't that honoring and serving God? Then they are holy."

"You make it sound like religions are all the same and they're not."

"Between religions, there are many more similarities than differences. They all identify when and how believers fall short of perfection (that's sin) and offer some means by which they can repent. They all teach ways of overcoming obstacles and negating temptations that redirect believers' flow away from good. And, all religions demand unwavering loyalty to a set of "sacred" laws. The differences are only denominational dogma."

"Yes, but both you and I know that like the saints, church people don't always adhere to the principles and laws. Sometime, act pretty much like they don't know what they are. There are plenty scriptures about a gossiping tongue, but what difference did that make to the saints?"

"You know what Dr. Talbin, if people fail to follow spiritual principles and laws, that should not be your concern. Afterall, they get the teachings, just like you do. Every religion teaches that punishments and rewards are meted out depending on the followers' degree of compliance with the common spiritual dictates. Obey, you find peace and joy. Disobey, you suffer."

"So you're trying to say that I didn't need to be concerned about the saint's gossiping, because...."

"Because by cutting yourself off from congregating with people in church who have righteous minds, you have been the only one punished. The saints probably repented and lived joy-filled lives. You were the only one burdened and for years, kept from experiencing your deepest spiritual joys. If you haven't already, forgive them and see what a difference it makes."

"Soooo Dramane, let me get this straight. You're saying that no matter what I see happening in church, I am suppose to just overlook it and forgive?"

"Nooooo, that's not what I'm saying. You are suppose to do what you can to make your hurt known to the person, then, forgive them. Let me clarify what I mean by forgive: You no longer allow the deed to negatively impact your life. To separate you from holiness."

"I know you said you are not, but you sound almost like a Christian preacher to me."

"Well you know I'm not. Oh, as far as the saints are concerned, regardless of what they said or did, you could have still found spiritual joy in some religious order. All you really had to do was work through the '3Ds. That is, discover what the religion espouses, decide whether or not you believe it and if so, do whatever needs to be done to follow its sacred principles and laws. As simple as it is, I have never understood why churches are filled with so much dissension and believers with so much animosity. Your joy or lack of it didn't have to rely on the saints.

Listening to Dramane, I often thought him to be what African traditionalists would call "an old soul who had returned." I was often surprised at the wisdom spouting from the mouth of this young man of thirty-eight years.

That night, Dramane's words excited every impulse of my nature long after he was gone. Over the next few days, I took each of my long-held distains for church and the saints and raked them over the coals of Dramane's insights one by one. Decided there were things I needed to do.

First, I needed to acknowledge my shortcomings. The only reason I had allowed the saints to stunt my spiritual growth, was that I expected people in the church to be perfect. I needed to accept that each person is where they are on their spiritual journey, not where I think they should be. Doing and saying what they do and say, not what I think they should do and say. They don't have to answer to me. This understanding made my soul expand with the strangest sense of freedom. My hostility toward the saints splintered into trash heaps and the cool breeze of clarity began "swooshing" them away.

For only the second time since I was a girl in Shetland, I tasted the warm elixir of spiritual joy. This time I swallowed. The warm after-glow gave me an overwhelming sense of belonging. It helped me begin the move out of my small hut filled with stored spiritual restrictions, into a mansion where I could harmoniously dwell even with those whose beliefs and actions were not what I judged they should be. I began surrendering my long-held, festerings for not only the saints, but Jane's father, Uncle Ray, Principal Rowell, the professors…in fact, I started writing a forgiveness list. Wouldn't you know? The opportunity to practice my newly heightened sense of forgiveness and inclusion presented itself the very next day?

In the afternoon, my doorbell rang. I could not imagine who it would be, since Khadia, my attendant, was sitting across from me. Dramane was still at work. When I answered the door, there stood an African woman greeting me in English.

"The guardeean told me thot a woman speakin' English leeves heah. I jes' wantid ta seh, 'ello," she said.

"If you have the time, come in. Khadia and I are just sitting," I answered.

I was as thrilled to hear Mme Wulu speak English as she seemed happy to speak it.

Mme Wulu's visit was shocking. Her conversation filled with warnings about the 'locals." She had come from a neighboring Country.

"You carn' trus' deem. Dey weel steel ev'eting an' eenyting dey carn. Dey're nasty, too. Don' let deem fool ya, eh."

Yes, my mouth was hanging wide open. I wanted to say something in defense of the locals, but my mind was racing so fast that I could not think clearly. Again the two, mind and mouth, would not cooperate. I was totally flabbergasted.

How can she be so hostile toward her own people?

Mme Wulu wasn't the only one hostile. Listening to the newscasts, I heard more than one story about locals who in mob fashion were harassing and beating foreign merchants. The merchants were not French, Belgian or even American, but other Africans from neighboring Countries who had come years before. They had invested their time, hard work and resources.

There were reports of businesses being burned and "Leave Out Now!" signs written on walls. There were even reports of the police stopping and intimidating drivers and passengers of vehicular convoys joined in exodus. A small City near the Capitol declared itself an independent Republic so it could pass laws against African foreign Nationals.

How could this happen? Can't they see? See they are all Black? All African? All human? What are they thinking?

Alright Robin ol' girl, slow down. Remember, people do and say what they do and say because of where they are on their spiritual journey. Some are not as mature as others. Focus. Focus. Instead of getting yourself all worked up about others, sit and work at improving your own thoughts and deeds.

Making my home in Africa would mean that I had to constantly deal with "genderism." Also with "xenophobia," tribe against tribe, much like the race against race back home.

How long before the hostility is directed at me? After all, I am a foreigner! I don't belong to either of the tribes indigenous to this area.

I sat and searched the recesses of my mind for my most helpful advisors of the past. I had crucial decisions to make and wondered what they would say. For the first time in a very long time, I heard "the voice."

Do you intend to search forever? Every time you think you have found that special place, ugliness rears its head and you're off searching again. When will you stop and take a close look at where it really is you have been searching for all these years. Africa was your last hope. Is it that you hope to find Sir Thomas Moore's Utopia? Hope to find a place where you will have the perfect family, perfect life? A place where everyone's intentions are pure?

When I considered what "the voice" said, I realized that nowhere would I find a family who was nurturing 100% of the time, or set of friends who required nothing more than that I just…"Be." People, places and circumstances would always make their demands. Would always require something from me.

Anywhere I go I will face some kind of challenge; have some kind of storm brewing on the horizon of my calm blue sky. Would I really want to live in a place like that even if I found it? A place of sameness would be boring; a place without…life.

If you really want to be happy, all it takes is a change of head, Canata's gentle voice reminded me. This time she added, *"Only in the quietness of a loving heart and reverent soul can you just… 'Be.'*

Well I certainly can't expect any place, anyone or anything to produce that for me, now can I? I am the one who will have to keep my heart filled with love and maintain a reverent soul.

The night I was helping Khadia pack my things, my thoughts bumped into Valley Girl. In her odd speaking style, she uttered life-changing words.

"Like Dr. Talbin girrll, you can go home anytime you want to. 'Cause home is like…wher-ev-vah! It's like wher-ev-vah you feel…like…you know," she said.

At first I just chuckled to myself, waving my hand in an "ah-stop-being-silly" motion. But later, I thought about valley girl's words and recognized their truth. Putting the last piece into my bag, I knew.

Home really is wherever! Wherever I feel a warm fit. Wherever I feel loving and peaceful at least most of the time. Shoot! My home can be wherever I want it to be!

By the time the fastener on my bag snapped, the discontentment that had for most of my life, gnawed at my heart and soul with its spiny little teeth, began to ease. Squeezing my ol' right hand, I whispered, "Here we go again. You and me" and got excited about the life of service, quietude and contentment I knew awaited me.

Oh! If I ever need somebody to listen, you are still there?

Right?

EPILOGUE

Robin felt the serene breeze. Cell after cell her once healthy, robust body transformed and drifted upward, upward toward what she had always called her "mighty kingdom." Her remembered world drifted farther and farther away. By now, it was all a blur.

Self and world no longer recognizable, Robin ceased looking back. Instead, she was content to peacefully float toward whatever was ahead.

Welcome, welcome, Robin sensed, but thought, W*ho is that? Where am I? Whatever will I do here?*

Again, *Welcome! Welcome!*

No longer feeling the need to question the greeting she sensed, Robin graciously acknowledged it.

Yo, yo, your stream is c-c-cleared. We, weee've been preparing it for, for, for a long, long time. Why, why were you so difficult, the first essence awkwardly asked. From another essence came the words, *We understand your need to know where you are and why you're here. We were brand new...once,* slowly and smoothly oozed into Robin's being like cream through cheese cloth. She felt the total presence of both essences in all time and space.

Don't, don't worry. You, you'll understand it all bet, bet, better by, by, byyyy and by. (Oooops! Maybe that wasn't allowed.)

Sensing the all too familiar refrain, Robin knew it would be of no benefit to question it. Living in the outer world had confirmed that there would be no answer. She also felt no need to launch her well-rehearsed, passionate response to the words that had before this very moment, always stirred her fury. Instead, she calmly headed toward her stream. There, she knew she would again be made whole.

Aaaaaah, this will be wonderful. No need to struggle, no need to question. No need to indulge in any negative sensibilities. At last, I can just..."Be." Can simply be fully part of the Flow.

Before she could wholly immerse in her stream, something happened on which Robin had not counted. Like a steady parade of melting dreams, her life began passing before her in review. The frame of each happening was as vibrant and clear as the sky, clouds and stars surrounding her. At first, she began traveling with them, but was pulled back by the words *Wha, what does?...(Oooo)... (Aaaah)...Oh why don't you just tell us what 'You'll understand it better by and by' really means,* the essences asked.

A response was clearly visible in Robin's mind.

Be patient. Understanding will come when the time is right, she thought. But blurted out, "You ain't got to worry 'bout a thang, 'cause the right answer gon' come."

Ooops! That was loud. But how was I to know I still had voice?

By the time Robin said the word "thang," her voice began to rapidly fade.

Hummmmmm. Maybe I need to save any voice I have left to say what I really want to say jes' one mo' time.

Rememberings of her lifelong search began its parade. But only one thing did she question this time.

I wasted a lot of time questioning everything, didn't I?

The answer was immediate.

I should have jes' recognized, accepted and shared truth whenever and wherever I found it, instead of spending all that time chasing and trying to capture the truth I desired.

What was generally Robin's questions, were now clear summations. Finally, she was at peace with everything that had happened in her past. And unlike before, she took pleasure in knowing there was no need to concern herself with what would happen next. The future would express…as it pleased.

"Ain't no need to worry 'bout nothin'. Ev'rythang is jeeees fine."

The sounds spewed in a crescendo, then quickly faded into a declining whisper. With the last issue of voice, also went the last of Robin's earthbound attachments.

She completely entered her stream.

The words, *Thank you so very much and I promise I will do better*, welled up as ascending, pure thought. The pure-thought promise somehow jiggled and set the stream into lightening-speed motion.

Robin felt no need to defensively shut her eyes, this time. The widening beam of light was wonderfully warm and soothing.

Without warning, multi-colored squiggles and showers of sparkles presented as if a speeding train had quickly, but silently applied its breaks.

Robin's stream slowed to a halt. She looked around in awe.

This can't be! Naaaw, this can't be! Is this the oval kingdom?

You know it is Godmother, why did you ask, the angel responded bearing a look of puzzlement.

Watch for these upcoming Fiction Memoirs in the

WOMEN OF SHETLAND Series

By

SANDI HOLLIS:

•GRACE IS SUFFICIENT

•SAVING MADAME DRAGON'S DESTINY

Attention organizations

All Personna Communication LLC books are available at quantity discounts with bulk purchase for educational, business or sales promotion use. For information please contact:

Personna Communication LLC

Special Markets Department

P.O. Box 23975

Detroit, Michigan 48223-0975

www.personnacom@aol.com

ORDER FORM

Please send the novel Finding Home (Book I)

From the

Personna Communication LLC fiction series

WOMEN OF SHETLAND

Quantity _____ @ $13.95= $_____

Sub Total   = _____

Sales Tax   = _____

Total Enclosed = $_____

____ To pay by check or money order, make payable to:

Personna Communication LLC

P.O. Box 23975

Detroit, Michigan 48223-0975.

____To use your credit click on Pay Pal @

http://HubBooks.homestead.com/womenofshetland.html

Please allow 2-3 weeks for delivery.

THE AUTHOR

Sandi Hollis is a fiction novelist, gifted with creative imagination. She says about her retirement from academia, "Now I can write the way I have always wanted since I was a little girl in Alabama." Her travels across the US, Africa and Europe chasing her dreams, have given her much about which to write. She calls Alabama, Michigan and Virginia home, but you will find her "wherever I receive insight and inspiration to write it."

The author would appreciate your comments. You can contact her by e-mail at: sandihollis@aol.com

Printed in the United States
R2024400002B/R20244PG43405LVSX00002B/1-12